BELIEVER

A CAMILLE BISHOP NOVEL

RAVIN TIJA MAURICE

Believer

Copyright 2019 by Ravin Tija Maurice

First Edition

Cover and Formatting

RMGraphX

10 9 8 7 6 5 4 3 2 1

ALSO BY RAVIN TIJA MAURICE

CAMILLE BISHOP

PROPHECY GIRL
BELIEVER

THE AFFLICTED SERIES

REBIRTH
IKON

To RM and Tara - love you boochies.

'You know that place between sleep and awake, that place where you still remember dreaming? That's where I'll always love you. That's where I'll be waiting.'
- *Peter Pan*, J. M Barrie

MY NAME IS CAMILLE BISHOP.
AND IF I DON'T WATCH WHAT I SAY,
I AM RIGHT, ROYALLY SCREWED.

Kiera dropped the file on the metal table, watching me without saying a word. The interrogation room had a weird chemical smell, which I assumed meant that it had been cleaned recently. I held up my handcuffed hands. "Is this really necessary?"

"Absolutely." She slid into the chair across from me.

My hands dropped to my lap. I flexed my fingers, slowly loosening the cuffs with magic, hoping she didn't hear the click. They were heavier than I expected when they were actually on, cold and very unforgiving when I tried to move my tiny wrists around which was why I was trying to loosen them. While I sat there, I saw a woman in my mind in a dark dirt cell with manacles around her wrists, in a long white robe. The whole scene felt very medieval.

Maybe trouble was a common thing for the *blanchmains.*

"You're lucky that the arresting officer recognised my last name," Kiera began, her face expressionless. She kept her dark eyes pointed down as she read the file, smoothing her pulled back hair with her right hand."You're lucky I caught it before anyone called Ted."

"Why would they call Ted? I *am* an adult. Don't forget." I went to point at her and stopped myself.

"Racketeering, possession, obstruction, withholding evidence in an open homicide investigation...."

"Obstruction and withholding? Seriously, Kiera? I told you I would give you Jesse's phone. It's not entirely my fault that we haven't connected. Possession is a joke. Test what I had. It was fucking *herbal tea* for Christ's sake. And I *love* racketeering. That is just adorable. If I was going to do anything even remotely like racketeering, do you think I would do it in a stinky ass restaurant in Chinatown like some dumb movie cliché? *God,* Kiera, give me some goddamn credit!"

"If they charge you, whether it sticks or not, you will lose your PI license. Are you ready to lose everything for some friend?"

I chuckled. "What *friend* are you referring to?"

"Bliss Fiori."

"*She is not my friend,*" I snapped. Kiera wasn't wrong; all this bullshit was because of her. Because I was the fool who tried to save her.

Kiera raised her hands in defeat. "Well, excuse me. The report says they also picked up a Philomina LeFaye. Is that any relation to your mother?"

"Yep. My mother's cousin."

"I love that you're trying to connect with the other side of your family, Cas, but if they are dragging you down the wrong path, I will have to step in." Kiera's use of my childhood nickname was a bit of a surprise, given the situation. Usually when someone was angry with me they called me Camille.

"It's not like that. They were helping me look for Bliss."

"Wait, I thought you said she wasn't your friend?"

"She's not. I thought she was." It all seemed so ridiculous now. I closed my eyes and massaged my temples without thinking. My eyes popped open as I hid them away, but Kiera didn't notice. "Something happened, and I was worried. She is sucked in with Tobias Kinkaid, and she's on drugs. But she told me to fuck off. I am done trying to help someone who doesn't want me around." There was no way that I could tell her the truth about my storybook life, and that vampires, viruses and magic actually exist. *Especially my magic.*

"Look, Camille, I know things have been rough for you since Jesse died—"

"Don't start with that shit either. Everything always goes back to stupid Jesse. *Jesse, Jesse, Jesse.* I feel nothing for Jesse. *Nothing.* Yet, he somehow still dominates my life even though he's dead. Bliss was the only female

friend I have ever had, so I did what I could to help her."
I pulled in a heaving breath and audibly let it out. "She's
exactly like Jesse. You can't save someone who doesn't
want to be saved. When and if—and that's a *big* if—she
is ready, she can come find me."

That wasn't entirely true either. The way Bliss ended
it; I wouldn't help her if she came to me.

"I'm done, Kiera. Can I go home? If you drop me off, I
can give you Jesse's phone. But you have to let Millie—I
mean Philomina out too. She was just there helping
me, that's all." I didn't tell her we had been with other
people. If she hadn't mentioned them, I assumed they
hadn't been picked up.

Hopefully, Eric had grabbed Nya and ran. I would call
him as soon as I got my phone back. He may not pick up,
but I would try.

"Funny, she said the same thing about you. Even
offered to pay your bail if the need arose."

As Kiera closed the file, I felt my expression brighten.
Millie was a good person. I was grateful to have her in
my life. Having her and Nya, and now Eric, made this shit
with Bliss almost bearable. At least I wasn't alone.

"I know there is more going on than you are telling
me, Cas. Why the hell are you even in the vicinity of a
Kinkaid? If he finds out you're a Bishop...."

"Kiera, I can tell you right now that me being a Bishop
is the very least of Tobias Kinkaid's worries." I looked
away from her as I said it, being sure to keep my hands
under the table in case they turned white at the mention

of his name. The overhead lighting gave them an eerie glow.

I wasn't even a blip on their radar. *Blanchmains'* maybe, but whether they knew that was me or not, I had no idea. The prophecy that gave me that title, and powers that made my hands glow whip cream white, were pretty new to me so it wouldn't surprise me if no one else knew what it was either.

If they realized they had murdered the *Blanchmains'* parents... well, that was a whole different shit show.

"Are you really that naive?" She wrote some things down in the file then closed it again. She fiddled with the end of her ponytail for a minute as she thought, something I remember her doing when we were kids.

I stretched my neck, straining my eyes to see what Kiera had written about me."What did you write?"

"That you were working a case and no wrongdoing was committed. The same thing I wrote in the LeFaye file."

Without thinking, I reached across the table and took her hand. "Thanks, Kiera."

"What the fuck is wrong with your hands, Camille?"

1.

THREE WEEKS BEFORE…

FOR THOSE AT HOME PLAYING ALONG…

OUR PLUCKY BUT RELUCTANT HERO HAS FOUND OUT SHE`S THE PROPHECY GIRL, AND HER TRUSTY SIDEKICK HAS BEEN KIDNAPPED BY A FLOCK OF IDIOT VAMPIRES.

SHE`LL RISK EVERYTHING TO SAVE HER FRIEND. BUT IF THEY FIND OUT WHAT HAPPENED TO THEIR SISTER, THE SIDEKICK WON`T HAVE LONG.

WILL OUR HERO SUCCEED? STAY TUNED…

My ringing phone was loud and obnoxious. I was immediately offended when I had to open my eyes. Through my clouded vision, I couldn't read the call display, I fumbled for the answer button, swiping it with my eyes half-open. "Yeah," I growled. I didn't care who it was.

"Cas?" Bliss whisper-shouted. "Cas? Can you hear me? Cas?"

"Yep. Sorry, I had fallen asleep. What's up?"

"The Kinkaid boys." My ears perked up. "They came to Ren and grabbed me. I think they are going to...."

I sat up, heart sinking into my butt. "Going to what? Bliss? Bliss, are you there?"

"I have the GPS and Bluetooth turned on on my phone. Track it and find me. But they may come after you, too, so watch your back. If I don't make it, promise me you'll run, Cas."

"What? Fuck that!" I shouted, clapping my hand against my thigh in punctuation. "I am coming for you, Bliss. I will call in the cavalry."

I heard yelling in the background. There was some shuffling, like the phone was in someone's pocket. I heard Bliss scream, and then the phone fell.

"Are you that retarded that you didn't check her for a phone?" a male voice yelled. There was a loud crunch just before the phone went dead.

"Bliss! Bee! Hello?"

Fuck.

The phone disconnected, and I couldn't inhale. Sitting at the edge of my bed, I put my feet flat on the ground and leaned over so my head was by my knees, finally able to take a calming breath.

I didn't know what to do. I put the phone down on my bed and stared at it, as if it would suddenly have all the answers, like a Magic 8 Ball. All the training in the world couldn't prepare a person for something like this. I thought about calling Kiera, but how would I explain it all?

Yeah, so, the Kinkaid brothers kidnapped Bliss. No, they had a good reason. They think Bliss killed their sister. Well, she did. But they don't know that for sure.

I couldn't call her people. Bucky was dead, and her mom would just call the cops. Should I hunt down Nico? I could call October, but with any of those options, I would still have to explain the unexplainable.

I picked up the phone and called the only person I could think of that wouldn't think I was a nutjob. She picked up on the first ring.

"Hey, Camille!" I was surprised she was so chipper, considering it was late.

"Hey, Millie. Sorry for calling so late, but I have a pretty serious problem," I began, taking a deep breath so I wouldn't cry. "The Kinkaid's have taken Bliss."

"Okay. Like kidnapped, or a 'poof' scenario? How do you know?"

"She phoned me. But they caught her, and the call ended. "

"Did you track her call?"

"Not yet. It literally just happened, and my head is a mess. Will they hurt her?"

"Track the call. I'll get in touch with my contacts and see what I can find out and call you back." She hung up quickly before I could say anything else.

I grabbed my laptop and, luckily, was still able to track the number.

Someone had not been paying attention. Tsk tsk. I expected more from mob children.

Google revealed that she had been taken to what could be best explained as posh suburbia. Parts of the outskirts of Toronto were lined with million-dollar homes with few neighbours around to ask questions. Using Google Earth I got a look at the house and the surrounding area in the daylight. But - even if she was still there - I had no vehicle, no team and no backup.

She had told me to run.

Where would I run to? I had nowhere to go. After some internal debate, I decided to call October. She had been there with The Wild Boys that night, maybe she could do something. Or, at the very least, could give me some ideas on what to do.

The phone rang three times before she picked up. "Well, hello there."

"Hi, October? It's Camille. Sorry to just randomly call you like this, but—"

"No need for the run around, Camille. Bliss pushed her panic button."

"Her what now?" I asked, a little mystified. I didn't

know Bliss had a panic button. It seemed odd, not only that October was at the other end, but that she would assume that I would know that. Saving that conversation for another day, I continued, "She called me before they smashed her phone. The Kinkaid's grabbed her. I am embarrassed to say I don't know what to do. With her brother being dead and—"

October snorted."Of course you don't know what to do. You're *just* a PI."

"Excuse me? I am so—"

"I have no time for you right now, little girl. I have a rescue to plan." And then she hung up.

Sure, I was pissed at what she said. I was *so* much more than just a PI. Getting into an argument with October wasn't going to help matters. If anything, it only costed us more time and made her mad at me. I was still sitting here and still didn't know what to do. Bliss needed me, and I couldn't help her. As the only female I had connected with as an adult, her friendship meant a lot to me. Sitting here and doing nothing while she was kidnapped by these knucklehead vampires for a crime they were not sure she even committed was *wrong*.

Why the fuck didn't I learn how to drive?

Fray could drive. But did I want to bring him into this? Even if we drove out there, I couldn't guarantee his safety. Or my own, for that matter. I couldn't guarantee anything. To anyone. And that fucking sucked.

I looked down at my phone. There was only one thing I could do. Put on my big girl pants. I printed out a map to the last location Bliss's phone had traced to, and then called a taxi. After changing into dark clothing with a black toque to hide my hair, I packed up my purse and snuck out the back door. The taxi picked me up down the street so Ted wouldn't see me leaving. Family asks a lot of questions when you walk out in the middle of the night dressed like a robber, and I was sure my Uncle would be no exception. And I liked living with him.

The house that her phone tracked to wasn't far, twenty minutes or so in the taxi. Which, if I remembered correctly, wasn't far from Bliss's mother's house.

The taxi let me out a few houses before the location. I would have looked like quite the asshole getting out of a cab right in front.

Driveways looped away from the street like they were their own versions of the yellow brick road. The grey brick roads led up to sprawling houses, the main difference to the Emerald City was the enormous trees that seemed to border every property, providing a small army decent cover and practically cloaked little old me. It was hard to tell in the dark, but it looked like there may have been woods and a ravine past the backyard.

Grey stone walls and a circular front drive made the house look like a fortress. It was completely dark, and the eerie quietness of the neighbourhood made my skin crawl. It all looked familiar for a moment but quickly went away.

I crept around the side of the property and was

genuinely surprised that there were no security lights turning on as I moved. But lights going on and off every time a squirrel ran by would be super annoying, and with all these trees there were bound to be lots of animals, so it made sense.

I was about to step out of the tree line when I stopped myself. In my tunnel vision to get here as quickly as possible, I had forgotten to check for cameras.

One above the front door, the back door, and the garage. And there were several large windows along the back of the house that someone would surely spot me from.

Trying to get inside the house was a bad idea. They could trap me like a caged animal, and that wouldn't help anyone. No one knew I was here. So if I got snatched, I was fucked. My stupidity smacked me in the face like a duelling glove, reminding me that I had really not thought this through. But I was desperate. And what did a good PI do when they were desperate?

I needed to improvise.

I dug deep into the energy welling inside me, moulding it into a hand that I used to throw all the cameras off angle, and then again to pick up a bunch of rocks and throw them through the back windows. I stayed hidden in the tree line, giggling to myself they exploded with a crash. The glass sounded a bit like hail as it fell on the concrete in tiny little pieces. I never knew that breaking so much glass could be so exhilarating.

It was a lot of noise. More noise than I had expected. I

hadn't thought about the neighbours hearing and calling the cops. Unless they were paid well to pretend to hear nothing. Or the houses were empty. Maybe the whole neighbourhood was empty.

What if there was a vampire nest in the basement? What if the Kinkaid's had some insane blood draining dungeon down there, with bodies suspended by their ankles as their life drained into a bucket below?

I waited and waited. No one came out. No lights turned on. Nothing. If someone was there, surely they would have sent security to check it out.

After a half hour of nothing, I decided to leave. There was nothing I could do.

As I walked away, I started to cry. This was some bullshit. I knew there was a good chance after they found her phone they would move her, but I had secretly hoped I was wrong. I wasn't about to go into a Kinkaid house alone and unarmed, so I couldn't even find a trail to pick up. I could do nothing else on my own. I called a taxi to a house on the next street over and headed back home.

An hour or so later, Millie called back.

"Sorry. It took me a bit to get a hold of my contacts," Millie said, and I heard shuffling in the background. "She's okay. And she will be, for the time being. I was told that one of the Kinkaid boys is in love with her and intends on claiming her."

"*Claiming* her? What the fuck does that mean?" It took everything I had not to yell.

"It means they want her as a mate. Whichever one it is wants her all to himself and is going to great lengths to do that."

"Well, we have to go get her! We have to *do something!*" I didn't tell her that I had already gone looking. The extent of my powers was supposed to remain hidden. No way would I let her know that I would sacrifice myself and this prophecy nonsense to get my friend back.

"I'm sorry, Camille. We could not find out where they were keeping her."

"I traced her cell phone. We could start there. If she's not there, burn the goddamn place down. Just so they know we're not fucking around. Then—"

"I know you're angry. I know you want to act. But that is not the way to deal with these people. She is not dead, and, as of now, there are no plans to kill her. My contact is trying to find out more. We have to wait until then to move on this. Can you do that?"

"But—"

"No buts, Camille. We will talk more tomorrow. Okay? Promise me you won't do anything stupid."

I exhaled loudly. "Alright. I won't. Your contact was sure they won't kill her?"

"Yes," she assured, "I will speak to you tomorrow. Try to get some sleep."

Yeah, that wasn't happening.

2.

I woke up late. I was amazed I had slept at all. There was a note from Uncle Ted on the kitchen table saying I had to make my own way because he was leaving early. I hurried up and got ready, texting him that I was running late.

I got on the subway and began my trek to work. Luckily, I had my mp3 player in my purse, so I could listen to music to pass the time. Like something out of a movie, the opening riff for 'I Knew You Were Trouble' by Taylor Swift came on, and Jesse stepped onto the subway car.

Or a dude that could have been Jesse's twin. Or clone. *Jesus*.

Except that wasn't possible because Jesse was dead. His blue, bloated face as it lay on a morgue slab appeared in my mind as if it was burned onto the back of my eyelids. The LeFaye had killed him because of me.

I gasped, sucking back tears.

I tried hard not to stare, but I found my eyes constantly going back to this man. If I had not known how young Jesse's little brother was, I would have thought it was him. An oversized sweatshirt seemed to cover much of his body, his hood pulled down enough that just the front of his scruffy blonde hair was sticking out. Baggy jeans draped over his not quite of the moment sneakers. His blue eyes were constantly darting around examining every possible mark or threat. I had a memory flash of us at sixteen, a sad gawky little me clutching his hand like a life preserver.

My heart continued to sink down, and my chest started to hurt. I did not miss him. It was his death that made me sad. Harold LeFaye and his people had killed him to jumpstart my prophecy; I would be a monster if I didn't feel the slightest bit guilty.

My greatest fear was that the person I was without him wasn't good enough. That his presence was the only thing that made me worthwhile. That I wasn't a person without him.

He didn't even look at me, this clone. I was happy and insulted all at the same time.

When I finally got to work, Ramona was busy on the phone. She smiled and waved as I went back to my office. I piled my bags on my desk and headed to the break room to get coffee.

Eric was stirring something in a cup when I walked

in. He looked different than when I had last seen him. He wore a faded black button-down shirt with the sleeves rolled up to the elbows, black jeans, and black boots. He had a watch with a thick leather strap that looked more like a wrist cuff.

"Good morning," I said, and he jumped as if I had startled him. He turned and smiled, his blue eyes twinkling.

"Morning," he replied. "There're donuts."

"Awesome!" I slithered in beside him and made a cup of coffee. I slipped a small plate off the shelf and grabbed four chocolate glazed.

I blushed when I saw his expression. "Sorry. I really need the sugar. Had a bit of a weird night."

"I'm not judging. Would it make you feel better if I told you this is my fourth coffee today?"

I smiled at him. "Actually, it would."

He was better looking close up. His vibe was almost magnetic, every move made me watch a different part of his body like I was studying it for further exploration. He was a man in so many ways, and the notion that someone like him, who was probably ten years older than me, would take a girl my age seriously was almost laughable.

"Hey, are you any good with Photoshop?"

"I get by. Why? You need some help?" I asked.

"I do. Can I come by your office later? You can give me a lesson?"

"Absolutely. Let me get settled, and I will let you know when I am free."

"Cool, cool." He waved a little as he left the break room, and I smiled all the way back to my office.

My phone was dinging when I closed my door. Repeatedly. I rushed to put my stuff down in case it was something important about Bliss.

It wasn't.

It was Kiera.

WHERE IS JESSE'S PHONE?

Before I could text back, Ramona paged me from the other phone. Her voice was low and flat. "Ted wants to see you in his office."

"Ruh roh."

"It's not like that, kid. But you need to go. Now."

I knocked on Ted's door and took his grunt as an okay to come in. He smiled a little too big as I sat down.

"Who died?" I asked. Pulling down my shirt so it didn't ride up as I moved, I sat sideways in the chair with my knees up over the arm rest.

"Why would you think someone died?" He chuckled awkwardly. I knew he was hiding something.

"Because you don't look at me like that unless something is up. Something that is going to bother me. Out with it."

"Kiera called—"

"She wants Jesse's phone. *I know.*"

"She wants Jesse's phone because it is evidence in a homicide investigation."

I hesitated. "Oh."

"Are you okay?"

"Yeah. Why wouldn't I be? It doesn't change anything. He's still dead. Do they have any leads?" My thoughts started to swim, and I didn't know what to say. I took a breath and tried to steady myself.

He stared at me. I did my best to keep my face blank and unreadable.

If I told him, he wouldn't believe me. I didn't want to think too much about the truth. Because in that version I was responsible for multiple deaths, which I had not fully come to terms with.

"She didn't say. She just said she needs that phone. Do you still have it?"

"Yes. I will get in touch with her as soon as I go back to my office." I stood up and went for the door, pausing and looking at him before I stepped out. "Right. Before I forget. You know Millie from the cafe down the street? Turns out she's my mom's cousin."

"Wait a minute! Wait a minute! Back up. Come back in here and sit down. This is a big deal, Cas. How did you find this out?"

I leaned against the doorframe, smiling weakly. "I vetted her. I was only able to sit and talk with her recently to corroborate. We're going to hang out. She's going to introduce me to her kid... kids? I forget now which she said. But anyways, it's cool. Sort of a silver lining type deal."

He smiled warmly. "Absolutely. I am extremely happy

for you."

"Great! I am going to go deal with this Kiera shit before it gets weird." I shuffled off towards the door.

"Are you sure you're okay, Cas?"

"Right as rain." I gave him a two finger salute, calling back to him as I walked out. "Now get back to work."

Jesse's phone was still in my purse. I had copied its contents to my laptop already, so I wasn't too worried about handing it over, but I was reluctant until Q got to take a look at it.

I texted Q and filled her in, letting her know what was happening and asking if she was coming by today so she could do her thing before I had to hand it over. Then I texted Kiera. I told her I had the phone and not to worry, she would have it asap. When I didn't get an immediate response back, I put my phone away. I was just about to get to work when there was a light knock at my door.

Eric poked his head in. "You got a minute? I could use some help."

"Messed up, right?" I could tell by his confused expression that he was looking at my desk.

He chuckled. "A little. But at least you've got a desk."

"You ready for the Photoshop help?"

He smiled. "Absolutely. But the conference room would probably be better."

I stood up and slid out from behind my desk, collecting my phone, coffee and donuts, and then followed him out.

His coffee cup was already waiting for us when we

walked in, so I put my stuff down beside his. Once we were settled, he turned his laptop towards me and showed me the picture.

"Lewis has got you doing the grunt work, huh?" I took a bite out of my chocolatey goodness. A quick thought of how I looked crossed my mind, and I became very self conscious of my appearance. With the back of my hand I brushed a few faded purple strands off my forehead and hoped for the best.

"I like it. It's paying my dues. I knew this job wasn't going to be glamorous. Photoshop doesn't want to cooperate though. It drives me nuts."

"You'll get used to it. It's really a matter of trial and error. I suggest fucking around with your own photos to see how certain functions work."

"That's good advice. Thank you."

"This one is a bit grainy, so we do this." I made a few adjustments to help balance the colours, then brightened it up. I took another bite of my food as I eyed the picture. "I see Mrs. Tanner was using us to hide an affair."

"Chris mentioned that. He just asked me to gather information about her. I haven't met her or anything. There is this weird thing she does though."

I smiled. "Define weird."

"Once a week, at midnight, she orders a large pepperoni pizza."

"Oooh, how scandalous!"

"That's not the weird part! She eats the *whole* thing— by *herself*—while sitting cross-legged in her underwear on the floor of her home gym." He took back his laptop, clicked on a few things, then turned back with a photo of Mrs. Tanner doing exactly what he said. It was hilarious and shocking.

"Well, I'll be damned. I am happy to know I'm not the only person who does that," I replied, and we both started laughing.

My phone rang, and I excused myself for a moment to answer.

"Hey, Camille, it's Millie. Sorry to call while you are at work," she began. I watched Eric in my peripheral vision to see if he was listening.

"It's no problem. I was just about to text you."

"I don't have much to tell you. My contact has gone AWOL so we need to go looking for her. We can gather more info as we do that." The hair on the back of my neck stood up. This was not good at all.

"Do you think they..."

"No. The Kinkaid's don't have many witches in their employ. They really don't want to lose this one."

"Why don't you tell me her name? I will see if I can find her."

"Alright. Her name is Lilly Darling. Don't get your hopes up. If she went poof, she won't be easily found. We'll be going out looking for her tonight. Are you coming?"

"Of course. Who is we?" I asked. I was dead curious.

"My daughter will be joining us. Do you know how to play poker?"

3.

Millie texted me later to say she would be by around 9PM to pick me up.

Figuring out what was an appropriate outfit for this occasion was not easy. What does one wear to go searching for a witch? So I picked out something simple, and transferred my essentials to a smaller purse. A sweater with longer sleeves that I could pull down over my hands was a necessity. My Mom's ring completed the outfit, and I was ready to go.

I didn't know where we were going, but part of being a good PI was being prepared for anything. And I was. Well, anything I understood.

Ted was in front of the television when I came downstairs.

"I'm going out with Millie and her daughter," I told him, leaning over his chair and kissing his head. His greying hair smelt like Old Spice and faintly like cigarette smoke.

"Oh yeah? Sounds cool. What are you guys doing?" He was nursing a beer and watching one of the various *Law and Order's*.

"No *Grey's Anatomy* tonight?"

He took a sip of his beer. "It's not on tonight. Have fun with your new family."

"Are you trying to be bitchy or was that an accident?" I sat down on the floor in front of him. "Because *you* are my family. You and Cuddy and all the Bishops who took care of me after my parents died. Millie and her daughter and anyone else with the last name LeFaye are just my mom's people. That's all. And I like Millie."

"I like Millie too." He leaned over and pulled me towards him, hugging me tightly. The smell of beer and his aftershave wrapped around me life a blanket. His body was warm, his cotton Ralph Lauren dress shirt was soft against my cheek.

He sighed loudly into my hair. "I am just worried about you. You are a little too calm and collected since Jesse died."

"I'm doing okay. Weren't you the one who said I am better equipped to deal with life than most people because of all the therapy I've had? Loving a junkie does things to your brain. You make peace with gnarly shit."

"I know. I just keep thinking if I were in your shoes, I would be a fucking mess," he said as he let me go. "Especially now that it's a homicide investigation."

"Should I call his parents? See how they are?"

"No. They may expect something of you that you

are probably not interested in doing. You are not the grieving widow." He kept his eyes on me, his dark brows giving a hint of what his hair once looked like. He had a distinguished look about him, like the private investigators from the old noir movies that wore trench coats and fedoras.

"Good point," I said as the doorbell rang. I stood up and kissed him on the cheek. I smiled at him, my hand resting on his shoulder. He smiled back at me, and in that moment I felt like everything was going to be ok. That was part of Ted's magic; his calm demeanour was a blessing after he took me in when my parents died.

I grabbed my stuff and headed for the door. "Don't wait up!"

I stepped out on the porch, locking the door behind me. It felt like I had closed off one world and was stepping out into a new one. Millie pulled me into a hug, and when she backed away, she asked, "How are you holding up?"

"I'm okay at the moment. The police have opened a homicide investigation into Jesse's death. Have you heard anything about Harold and his people?"

"No. Oddly enough, I haven't. But I'm sure I mentioned before that they are an isolated group."

"Well, my cousin Kiera is on the case. They better have covered their asses or what's left of them are going to jail," I said as I followed her off the porch. Her black SUV was parked right out front.

"What's left...?"

She got in the driver's seat and unlocked the back

door so I could get in. A young, petite woman sat in the passenger seat; she looked a little older than me. Her dark brown hair was cut in a cute short bob with bangs that was glossy and beautiful. She smiled at me, and I couldn't help but smile back.

"Camille, this is my daughter Nya. Nya, this is Camille. Now, you were saying something about what's left?"

"Can I speak freely?"

"Yes, of course. You're safe with us."

"Okay. When I had that altercation with Harold and them, I took a few of them out. They told me they killed Jesse because I am some 'prophecy girl', and I flipped out. I used my powers—for the first time I might add—so I didn't know what I was doing, and I killed Harold's wife along with a few others."

"How did you pull that off?"

"Well," I began, looking down at my hands. "These things came out of my hands, the best way to explain them is like strands of energy and power that looked, to me, like threads and attached onto them. These threads stuck themselves to a deeper part of the person, like plant roots digging into soil. In a burst of anger, which is understandable because they were threatening me and Bliss, I pulled on them. When I did it was like I pulled their essence out of their bodies. What came out of Harold's wife was like a puff of smoke. My hands also turn super white and it's freaky as shit. I'm scared what will happen to my brain when I process what I have done, and what I can do."

"Have you summoned anyone yet?" Millie asked.

"Not that I am aware of."

"Have you ever had a dream where you felt like the person was really there? Like it was super real, and you woke up confused?" Nya asked.

"Um... yeah. I have. That was summoning?"

"A form of it. Some spirits choose to come forward that way because it's easier on the person and easier for the spirit to communicate on that plain of existence."

"Does this mean I can talk to my mom? To both my parents?"

They both were silent.

"We don't know. So we're not going to comment. There is a possibility, but there are no guarantees. Magic doesn't work that way," Millie's tone was very to the point. "We need to prepare you for where we're going. This is not your uncle's poker game."

I chuckled. "You would probably be shocked if I told you about some of my uncle's poker games. Ted's the *good* uncle."

"You have to keep your temper down. We're not walking in there to prance around *Blanchmains* like a prized pony, if you catch my drift. If you see someone use their powers, you have to act like business as usual. Same if there are any 'others' there. Got it?"

"Got it. I'm good. I promise," I told them.

"You know, if you don't mind me saying," Nya began, "You have handled all this really well, Camille. You're so calm and collected when you're talking about pulling essence out of someone's body."

"Nya!" Millie slapped her arm.

"What? If I was in her shoes, I would be bugging the fuck out. Like, postal." Nya smiled back at me. "Sorry! I'm good at putting my foot in my mouth."

"Hey, I think it's genetic. You and I are going to get along real well," I told her with a laugh.

"That is a good question. How are you feeling about all this, Camille?" Millie asked.

"Truthfully? It's weird. It's really fucking weird. It explains *a lot* of strange shit that happened to me after my parents died, but the fact that all this even exists is off the wall," I said. "I am dealing, but not. It's complicated."

"Well, buckle up. Because this is a whole new world." Nya laughed a little too hard, and her expression made the hair on the back of my neck stand up. She began to hum "A Whole New World" from Disney's Aladdin as we drove.

Chinatown, in downtown Toronto, was a brightly lit, colourful wonder of noises and sounds that seemed to never sleep. Even closed, stores were still lit up with flashing lights that glowed like they were in Technicolor. There were always people everywhere, even in the middle of the night; different ages, races, and styles of people that you wouldn't see in other neighbourhoods.

Millie parked in a pay parking lot, and Nya went and got a ticket from the machine.

"You guys want some money?" I asked.

"No need. Watch." Nya put in ten cents then waved her hand across it. The numbers shifted and turned from six minutes until the same time tomorrow.

"Cool," I blurted out. She put the ticket on the dashboard, locked the car, and we all started walking. The bustling streets were amazing and lively. I had to be careful to avoid the street vendors and markets that spilled their wears out onto the sidewalk, whether they were jewellery or fruit or a combination of just about everything. Even the smells competed for your attention, a mash of so many things that I couldn't tell whether they were pleasing or gross.

"Don't get any ideas about using it on a bank statement. It doesn't make money appear, it only changes images on a page."

I was going to say, "I wouldn't anyhow," but stopped as we came to a halt at a flight of stairs leading down to a brightly lit restaurant. A pink and green neon sign flashed above the doorway.

Nya put her hand on my arm before we could start down. "Listen, I know this is all new for you and shit, but please try not to stare. You're going to see some things that will probably shock the hell out of you. You can bug out about it another time. Alright? Whatever happens, play it cool."

"Dude, I'm a PI. Keeping my game face on was a course I had to take in college." I heard Millie laugh from beside her as I spoke. "I know I've been downplaying my whole epic unbinding by Harold, but I have to tell you, if I kept my cool during that shit, there isn't much you could throw at me that would shock me."

Millie laughed again. "Is that a challenge?"

I followed the two of them down into the restaurant. It was busy, with lots of loud voices and big round tables full of people and food. Some of the dishes looked amazing, brightly coloured vegetables with an array of meats and garnishes that was mouth watering.

"Are we going to eat?" I asked quietly as we headed to the back. "Because the food smells awesome."

At the back of the restaurant, a small, elderly Asian woman with pure white hair sat in front of a black curtain holding a long wooden cane with a silver handle. What appeared to be a wolf's head poked out of her claw-like grip.

The woman smiled at Millie. Her expression darkened when she saw me. She gestured towards me. "Who's that?"

"My niece, Camille. Camille, this is Madam Vo. This is her place," Millie said with a smile.

Madam Vo eyed me, looking me up and down a few times before motioning to the curtain behind her.

Millie handed the older woman something as we went by. She poked Nya with the head of her cane, it was definitely a wolf's head.

"No repeats of last time, or I will ban you." She scowled.

Nya smiled. "You have my word, Madam."

She rolled her eyes and turned back to the crowded restaurant. Nya took hold of my wrist and pulled me along behind her.

We went down a small hallway that led to a big back room where a group of people were gathered around another large round table. They were playing poker. A cloud of smoke rested just above the ceiling; smoking was illegal inside restaurants. Maybe this establishment was exempt.

All eight people looked up from the table and smiled at us, and I felt something twitching in my hand. I looked down at my ring, and my finger was turning white. Thin white lines ran from my hand up my arm.

"Good?" Nya asked as I pulled my sleeve down over my hand.

"Uh, yeah. Just no weirdness, okay? I can promise to keep my cool, but my hands will give me away. I can't control the... the... I don't know what the fuck to call it other than 'whitening,'" I whispered in her ear.

We crossed the room and grabbed some chairs. Nya and I sat down next to a tall, thin woman with super long hair. Millie went to the back of the room to talk to a group of people gathered in a corner. I tried to side glance at them so I could be aware of everyone in the room.

"Evening, Nya," the woman said. "Surprised to see you here."

"Evening, Bex. How's your night going?" Nya asked.

"Meh. You guys looking for info or something? Your mom doesn't usually talk to the chain gang."

"We are. But I don't know if you want to get involved."

Bex smiled. "Awww, c'mon. I am always down for a shit storm!"

"Okay. What do you know about the Kinkaid virus?"

Bex began to laugh. When she turned her head, I saw that the tips of her ears were pointed, and that her eyes were quite round.

"Virus? Oh, sweet pea. There are so many conflicting stories about that. You need to talk to the traitor herself."

Nya groaned. "Fuck. She's involved?"

"Who?" I asked.

"She works for them. She is their bitch," Bex sneered. I was taken aback by her reaction.

"Would she know if they were holding someone?" Nya asked.

Bex hesitated. "Not sure. Why? Who they got?"

"My cousin's friend got snatched. Mom's peeps told her that one of the knuckleheads wants to claim her."

"If they grabbed her friend and intend on claiming her, there is not a whole lot you can do about it. Except pray she ends up being food."

"Great. So where is the traitor? We should have a word with her."

"Apparently, she ghosted. Wanna guess why? You'll get a kick out of this one, being le Fay and all." She leaned in towards us, speaking quietly, "I heard she had a premonition about the rise of *Blanchmains.* It scared her so much she took off, and no one can find her. Is it true? Has *Blanchmains* happened? Everyone is saying it's true."

Without thinking, I sat on my hands. I would have to get a pair of gloves if this was going to continue. My stomach dropped. My anxiety went through the roof. I paid attention to my breathing and kept it calm. Millie and Nya had warned me not to freak out about what I saw, but nothing about what I should do if someone found out what I was.

"Not that we are aware of," Nya told her. "Oh, this is my cousin Camille. Camille, this is my girl Bex."

I smiled and tried to breathe normally. "Nice to meet you."

"Likewise. I hope you find your friend, or they kill her. Being claimed is no way to live." Bex turned back to the poker game. I wanted to cry and puke at the same time.

Out of the corner of my eye, I thought I saw someone on the other side of the room. I fully turned and looked, studying carefully to see if the man I got a glimpse of was Eric. If he had randomly followed me here, this could be *bad.*

Really, really bad.

But the man faded into the shadows, disappearing into a dark corner of the room like he had never existed. All the shadows seemed normal and didn't change shape, I watched for a few minutes just to be sure. This wouldn't be the first time the dark played tricks on me, but now I may have an explanation. I looked around for Millie, who was still in the corner talking to the people Bex had called the chain gang. It seemed as if no one had noticed this person but me. Best case scenario I was being paranoid. Which was totally possible.

I have to calm down. No wigging out.

Something happened in the game that I didn't quite catch, then suddenly the entire table disappeared, including everything that was on it.

I tried not to seem startled, but when I saw some of the player's faces, I knew I wasn't the only one who was confused.

"Alright, who's the mook?" Bex yelled. "We're trying to have a fair game here!"

The table reappeared, and Bex threw her cards down. "We need to restart the hand! That is some bullshit."

"How do we know you didn't do it?" a man on the other side of the table asked. He wore an old Blue Jays baseball hat and a dark hooded sweatshirt. His face remained partially hidden, but I could see his large hands clenching into fists.

"Unless I got a major power upgrade, I *can't* do that, dummy. You probably did it and are trying to make me look like a douchebag. Well, fuck you," Bex stood up and began pointing at each player. "Fuck you. And especially fuck you." The cursing that came out of her mouth made me blush.

Madam Vo appeared in the hallway and slapped her cane on the floor. The whole room shook.

"Watch your mouth, young one." She gestured to Bex with the wolf head of her cane. "Any more and you're out."

Bex raised her hands in defeat, sitting back down.

The hand was dealt again, and everything returned to normal.

"Is this normal?" I asked Nya.

She laughed. "Just another day at the office." She turned back to Bex. "So what do you believe about this Kinkaid virus, Bexie?"

"Truthfully? They're making a play to take over the world and weeding out the weak. It's fucked up, it's like ethnic cleansing," Bex said. "I don't know if that's the *real deal,* but whatever it is, it's going to get worse before it gets better."

"So you think they won't kill my friend?" I asked Bex. She glanced at me, and then looked back at her cards for a moment before turning to me. Her perfectly circular green eyes looked like they were made of glass, hand painted with different shades that gave them an eerie glow.

"Do you think one of them is in love with her?"

A memory of the weirdness at Ren with the Kinkaid's played in my mind. "I think they think they are, but it's a twisted obsession thing. And it's all of them, including Lucia. She's a stripper."

"Sounds like a trophy. Do they all like her? Could be some weird power play."

"They also think she knows what happened to Lucia Kinkaid." That got their attention.

"*What happened to Lucia Kinkaid?*" Bex and Nya asked in unison. A few heads turned, but only for a moment.

"I don't know. It was something Bliss said when

she was able to sneak a phone call. I guess they think something happened to her. Why? No one has heard anything?" I asked, fumbling a few of my words. I tried to be as vague as possible, hoping my panic would be written off as concern for my friend.

Millie came over and pulled up a chair beside us. Nya nudged her mother. "Did Camille mention that something *may* have happened to Lucia Kinkaid? That they think her friend knows something?"

My mind went totally blank. I could not remember if Bliss and I had told Millie the truth about what had happened or not when we went to the Whistlestop after all hell broke loose.

"She did mention it. Have you met Lucia, Cas?" Millie asked.

"Yes, I have. I met all of them one night at Ren. That's the club my friend works at."

Bex chuckled. "Well, *that* explains a few things. There's another girl there that dances that...never mind."

"There is nothing going around about Lucia, but the traitor is definitely missing," Millie said with an exhausted huff. She sat back in her chair and crossed her legs, moving her long dark hair back behind her shoulders. From her stature and the way she composed herself you could tell that Millie meant business. Beautiful but tough as nails; something that I hoped to be. She smiled at me when she saw that I was watching her.

"Who is the traitor?" I asked.

Bex looked confused. "Is she new?"

"A little," Millie began. "There are five noble magic families. We're one, and the traitor is from another. By going to work for the Kinkaid's, she has betrayed us, in some people's eyes."

"Why?" I asked.

"Because they treat us like we're the scum of the earth. Like we're lesser beings because we're not vampires."

"What's her story? Maybe she has a good reason."

"Her name is Lilly Darling. She's a...." Millie turned her head away for a moment. "I am not entirely sure how the Darling's became a noble family, probably to shut them up. It is hard for them to prove their backstory because it is marketed as fiction."

"The same argument could be made about us."

"Not really. There is some evidence that Arthur could be a real person. Therefore, logically, the rest could be true. The Darling's claim lineage to *Peter Pan*."

"You have got to be kidding."

"I wish I was. The 'story' is that Wendy and Peter hooked up. A little young, I might add. They had a few kids, and after Wendy lost her marbles, they were fostered by Tiger Lilly, who was a powerful sorceress. The kids had inherited shadow magic from Pan, and after getting together with Tiger Lilly's kids, they developed a wide array of powers. Pan's shadow magic is the only dark magic that I am aware of that could rival... *Blanchmains*."

"So, is the story about *Blanchmains* true?" Bex asked Millie.

Nya smiled at her mother. "Story is that the traitor

split because she had a premonition about the rise of *Blanchmains*."

Millie's eyebrows raised. "Oh yeah? Well isn't that amusing. I guess we should be on the lookout. Especially since this is the first I have heard of Lilly Darling having premonitions, and I have known her since she was a toddler."

"I guess we should." I tried to be calm, but inside I was planning my hasty exit. "Did you find anything out?"

"A little. Bliss's fine, by the way. And she will be. Tobias Kinkaid intends to claim her. Word around town is that she is his chosen mate."

I felt like all the air had been let out of my body. All I could think of was Tobias's gooney face and how much I wanted to punch it. It was hard to believe that he was the same guy who was so drunk he broke a glass and cut up his hand one night when I was waitressing at Ren. That moment changed everything.

They weren't going to kill her. So that was good. But being claimed by Tobias Kinkaid….

"I have to find her. I have to try to rescue her. She won't want to be claimed. That's insane. She is in nursing school." I didn't even know where to begin. Bile began to rise in my throat.

Maybe I did need to talk to Kiera. Bliss had said that she was so deep undercover that Kiera wouldn't even be able to find her. Should I test that? She had to have a contact, someone she reported back to. If she was gone, it would set off alarm bells. But this could all just be part of her plan, a plan that she didn't—and probably couldn't—clue me in on.

Millie put her hand on my arm. "I know. Don't worry. We'll get Bliss back."

She looked at my arm, and her eyes widened for a split second. I was still sitting on my hands, but my wrists were a little exposed. I assumed because of her expression that meant they were white. Mille moved her chair closer to me, trying to arrange herself so her arm blocked one of mine.

I took a deep breath. I tried to calm and centre myself, but my head was swimming with thoughts of Bliss in chains, curled around the ankles of Tobias fucking Kinkaid.

I need a drink.

We stayed at Madam Vo's for a few hours, eating and chatting with other people. The food was fantastic. Luckily my hands went back to normal so I could eat.

It seemed a lot of people had heard about Lilly Darling taking off, and her premonition.

"Frankly, I hope it's true," Blue Jays hat-wearing man said when the topic came up.

"What? That the traitor ghosted? Don't we all. Maybe she went back to Never Neverland," Bex joked.

"No. I hope that *Blanchmains* is real," he continued. I sat on my hands again, trying to make sure no one noticed.

"Why do you care?"

"Because I like the idea of someone who scares the

shit out of the cabals. A magical messiah, if you will."

"Why would she scare the cabals?" I asked. People were startled, shocked to hear my voice. What a cabal was wasn't important at the moment.

"*Because of what she can do*," he grumbled. "Aren't you le Fay? You should know better than anyone."

I shrugged my shoulders. "My mom never talked about it."

"Scaring the cabals doesn't mean shit if she doesn't have people behind her. The le Fay are not enough on their own." A white-haired man turned from his place at the table, he resembled a modern-day Gandalf with his long white hair and beard and Slayer t-shirt."If she is around, tell her we're with her, Millie. Tell her if she wants to be the goddamn messiah, we are behind her."

Millie smiled. "I appreciate that. Unless I am super out of the loop, it is just not true."

One of the chain gang came over to us. She had long red hair, similar in colour to Ramona's, that flowed like it was alive when she walked. She stood beside us, smiling down at me from her place beside Millie. A strip of her hair coiled itself around her arm like a snake.

"We really hope you find your friend, dear," she told me. Her hair began to move on its own, slithering up her arm in its coil.

It brought tears to my eyes. Millie put her hand on my knee, and I took a deep breath and tried to remain calm.

I kept to myself for the rest of the night. I smiled and was friendly, but kept my hands firmly planted under my butt.

No matter how comfortable I got with these people, I could not let them know what I was. Just because they said they were down with *Blanchmains* didn't mean they would be when the chips were down. I had never felt so alone in a room full of people.

Another one of the chain gang approached us as we were walking out the door to leave. He was in his mid-50s and had longer hair that he pulled back into a sort of man bun, but he looked like the type of man that would never be mocked for his hairstyle. His well-muscled physique was obvious through his shirt. He smiled at me and was ruggedly handsome. Millie blushed when he came over to us. She tried to hide it, grinning ear to ear like a school girl.

He handed me his business card. "Don't hesitate to call if you need anything."

When I took the card, there was still a tiny bit of white around the ring on my finger. He saw it, then winked and nodded at me.

"Thank you, I appreciate it," I said. He walked away, and we left the restaurant.

"Liam Fitzpatrick?" I said to no one in particular as we walked down the street. I was examining the business card; all it had was a name and a phone number. No business name, logo, nothing else. Chinatown continued to pulse around us like a bright neon star. People were still out walking around, even though most things were closed except a few random restaurants.

Millie blushed again and grinned, lowering her eyes. I put a hand on her arm.

"For real? You and him?" I could not help but smile. "That was the Fitzpatrick you mentioned? I see what you mean."

"I wish there was a me and him," Millie sighed, her face glowed at the mention of him."He knows the full deal, about you I mean. He is a powerful ally, and he will keep your secret."

"So, he's a…a werewolf?"

"Not just a werewolf, but the alpha of the Fitzpatrick clan. He could sense something about you, and I know he is trustworthy. I wonder if anyone else could sense what you are."

I shrugged. "I wish I had talked to him."

"You will. One thing at a time."

"So what do we do now?" I asked as we started walking again. I had to be careful to avoid some of the garbage on the street. There were less and less people as we walked back to the parking lot, and I tried to be more aware of our surroundings. It wasn't unheard of for people, especially women, to get robbed in this neighbourhood at night.

Nya had her phone out and was scowling. She had been on it since we left the restaurant.

"You good, Nya? What's wrong?"

Nya waved at me like she was brushing me off. "You want answers? We need to find the fucking traitor. We need to talk to Lilly Darling."

4.

The next day at the office, I watched Eric. I was waiting to see if he was who I had seen last night.

Who? Or what?

But everything was business as usual. All that staring at him gave me a chance to see how cute he actually was. I loved the way his hair framed his face, drawing attention to his penetrating gaze. The slight hint of stubble, giving his jawline even more definition; it was calling me to touch it. He stood with the presence of a warrior, his well-muscled hands an implement of his strength. The pull was strong, and I hoped I could compose myself so I could carry on a conversation with him. The fact that he would probably never take me seriously didn't matter. *Yet*.

Maybe I wasn't giving myself enough credit.

He smiled at me as I sat by the break table and watched him, daydreaming as I held my coffee.

"Hey there," his voice snapped me out of my trance. "Everything good, Camille?"

"Five by five," I replied. Before Eric could get a chance to continue, I blurted out, "By any chance, were you in Chinatown last night?"

Something flickered in his eyes when we made eye contact, and his pupils dilated slightly. The edges of his mouth tilted up slightly like he was going to smile but didn't.

"No. Why? Were you?" he joked.

"Yeah. I thought I...never mind." I waved him off and took a sip of my coffee. Either he was a damn good liar, or I was being paranoid.

Eric sat down next to me and sipped his coffee. After a few minutes of uncomfortable silence, I spoke.

"Did you get those issues with Photoshop figured out?" I asked.

"Yeah, I think so. I still haven't figured out exactly what Mrs. Tanner is up to."

I smiled. "You may not. It may be Lewis who shows it to you. Sometimes these things aren't so easy to spot, and it takes someone more experienced to see it."

"Has that happened to you?"

I shrugged my shoulders. "Sort of. Lewis did point out to me that Mrs. Tanner could be using the situation as a way to hide her own affair. She came in originally and met with me about a stalker."

"Huh. I will have to take a second look at the evidence I gathered with that in mind. Maybe I missed something.

Thanks for the tip."

"Anytime." My phone beeped a few times from the table, and I briefly glanced at it. It was Kiera. Whatever it was could wait until this moment with Eric passed. Just in case I didn't get another one for a while. Or at all.

"I won't keep you." He stood up, adjusting his grey button down shirt. "We'll chat more later."

We smiled at each other, and then he walked away.

Good gravy he's cute.

I didn't check my phone until I got back to my office. Kiera had texted after she just called. It said **CALL ME NOW**! I didn't want her getting really angry with me, so I called her from the landline.

"Where the fuck is the phone, Camille?" she snapped at me when she answered.

"It's in my purse. Chill out. I am at the office if you want to come get it. I didn't know this was considered a homicide until you told me in the last few days so I didn't think it was an issue. You don't normally take two weeks to decide."

"I don't have time for this shit. Is the battery toast?"

"Nope. I charged it as soon as I got it."

"Who had it before you?"

"His idiot friend Rollo. According to him, someone found it in a garbage can at a bar downtown. He collected it from them when Jesse was still missing, I believe."

"What bar?"

"Don't know. The last picture is a bathroom selfie.

That might help."

The picture flashed in my mind, how terrible he looked in those final moments. I didn't want to remember him that way, all strung out and shitty looking. A pang of guilt went through me, and then I remembered Amanda, and it went away.

"Send it to me right now."

"Alright. Just—"

"Now, Camille!"

"Can I open my laptop, Kiera? Jesus."

"Can't you send it directly from his phone? Why are you opening your laptop?"

"I copied the contents of his phone to my laptop when I got it just in case. If the battery charge hadn't held, I wanted to make sure we were covered."

She hesitated. "That was smart. My boss is riding my ass because of the family connection. It's aggravating, considering the direction the evidence is going. But that stays between us. I am super stressed. Send me the phone contents. All of it. It will save me coming to get it for a little longer."

"Why would you need it at all then?"

"The GPS and Bluetooth. Techie needs access to the actual chip."

"I did not know that. Thanks for the tip."

"Send it. Right now."

"Putting it in a zip file and sending it now. Calm down."

"I will when we find out what the fuck happened to Jesse. I am trying my best to tell these morons that you were not together so questioning you is pointless, but it might not work forever. They may want to talk to you. Send me a list of his known associates and any details on them you think I need. And the ones you don't. I also want those videos you mentioned. From the brothel. Tell Ted and your tech."

"Will do." I texted Kiera's email to Q and told her to send the video to her. "Hey, Kiera, can I ask you something? Why *is* Jesse's death being investigated as a homicide?"

"The short answer that I can actually give you? Jesse's cause of death was left as undetermined. There were two autopsies performed. The second one found something that would suggest homicide. The two weeks were spent running tests. And just an FYI, you also may have been listed as his next of kin, but now that his parents are involved, you have no legal binding to him that you would be kept in the loop. I just did that as a courtesy."

"Well, okay then." I wasn't sure what to say about it, I couldn't exactly argue with her about his relationship with his parents, nor did I want to. "I will provide you with whatever info I can."

"Good. Maybe my boss will stop riding my ass. Talk to you later, kid." She hung up before I could say anything else.

I stared at the phone in shock—something I felt like I was doing a lot lately. I quickly hung it up, dropping it like it was something gross. I hadn't even entertained the idea of being questioned by the police about Jesse's death.

How would I explain my drive-by breakup to a homicide detective?

I crawled out from behind my desk and went to Ted's office.

"This feels like weird Deja vu," I said as I closed his door behind me.

"Explain." He kept his eyes focused on his laptop.

"Was I not just in here talking about Jesse's murder case?" My question made him perk up and look at me. He looked tired, the bags under his eyes a little darker than normal. I'd asked him why he didn't dye his hair to match his eyebrows, and he said that he liked the salt and pepper. It reminded him that he'd lived through some shit.

"What about it?"

"I talked to Kiera. Sent her the contents of his phone, which she is going to come get at some point. She wants you to send her that evidence you got from the brothel. She asked for Q's video too." I sat down across from him. "I had totally brain farted on the idea that they might want to question me. But they might. This is weird.""

"So? That's not a big deal. You have nothing to hide."

"Oh? I GPS tracked the victim's phone and caught him in a brothel. Then my friends and I tracked him *again,* so I could set up what would appear to be a random encounter to break up with him. Isn't that something to hide?"

He groaned. "I forgot about all of that. You can't mention Q's name to a detective. *Cannot.* Under pain of torture. I do like the idea that you guys are becoming friends though."

"I won't. What about the rest?"

"They might not handle the illegally obtained video well. Let me talk to Kiera."

"Cops have a funny way of making things work when they need to, don't they?"

He stopped what he was doing, pushed his laptop aside, and looked me dead in the eyes. "What's going on?"

"What do you mean?"

"They will catch who did this to him, Cas. And they'll figure out what happened to your friend's brother too. You can trust Kiera. You know that. How is Bliss holding up?"

"She's alright, I think. I haven't heard from her in a few days."

"Is everything good, Cas?"

I dug my nail into my palm to stop myself from tearing up. I wanted to tell him. I really did. He was always my safe space. I knew no matter what happened he would take care of me. I would be okay as long as I had my Uncle.

"Yeah, Ted. I'm good."

I got a text from Millie a few hours later, saying that she had gotten word of another poker game, and Lilly Darling might be there. I told her I was down to go.

Should I ask why there is so much poker playing going on?

I didn't see Eric for the rest of the day, and I found that I was a little disappointed. I barely knew him, but I wanted to know more about him. I hadn't ever wanted to spend time getting to know a guy before; it had always been all about Jesse. This was a new feeling for me.

I was thinking about Eric on my way home with Ted when Obsidian Butterfly came on the radio.

I turned up the volume a little. "This is Noah Fray and his band. Did I tell you that?"

"It came up, but we probably didn't discuss it. Have you seen him lately?" Ted asked, and my heart sank.

I had sorta agreed to be Fray's girlfriend, and now... now I wasn't so sure what I felt. It wasn't like he had called me lately. As a matter of fact, I hadn't heard from him since that morning I split from his place to go to the doctor. Which was also the same morning I saw a girl leaving his place while I had slept in the bedroom.

"No. It's been a weird couple of days. With Jesse's funeral and Bucky being dead, it's just been like the world is spinning a bit too fast."

"Your mom's family popping up must be weird too."

"Yes and no. Millie and her daughter are cool. I am going to see them again later, by the way. But they told me some stuff I wanted to ask you about. Do you know anything about my mom's parents? Her siblings?"

He thought for a moment. "She said her parents were dead. And there was something about a brother, but that was it really."

"Well, apparently, they're not dead. Scratch that, my *grandfather* is not dead. My grandmother passed recently, but he is still around. Along with my mother's *sisters.* Can you believe that? Millie said there was a falling out where my mom disowned them or something."

"Whatever it was, it must have been serious. Did Millie say...?"

"No. She doesn't know why. I told her that I have no interest in seeing them or speaking to them. If Mom didn't want me around them, I am sure she had a good reason. I will respect her wishes."

"I know that may seem weird, but I think it's the right thing to do. She was a pretty level-headed woman, your Mom. If she disowned them, it must have been for something she couldn't get past," he paused, watching my face in the rear-view mirror. "Did you look into them?"

I shook my head. "Nope. If I am respecting her wishes, I don't want to know."

"Do you want me to look into them?"

I thought about it for a minute. It would be a way to check in and see the aftermath of...of what I had done. Ted could find out if there were police reports, and shit that I couldn't easily get access to. Knowing Ted, I was surprised he had not done it sooner, even if he was respecting my Mother's wishes.

"Sure. But I don't want to know unless it's serious. Normal bullshit I don't care about."

"I can't imagine I would ever be able to find out why your mom disowned them."

"Of course." I laughed. "I know that. But you might, depending on what it was."

I wanted to tell him. *Soon enough, I may be able to ask her.*

Millie and Nya came by after dinner. Ted was still in the kitchen cleaning up with Cuddy. Watching the two of them interact always made me smile because even though there was some teasing and silly comments, there was so much love. Ted loved his son like no one else, and Cuddy worshipped the ground his father walked on. I always wondered if my parents were like that with me, but I was never jealous of what my Uncle and cousin had because it was beautiful.

"Millie, you know Ted. Ted, I wanted you to meet Millie's daughter, Nya, and both of you to meet my cousin, Cuddy." I smiled. "Cuddy, this is Millie and Nya. They're my mom's people."

Ted looked surprised when he saw Millie, who was dressed in a black leather jacket, tight jeans and knee high boots with a heel. With her dark hair flowing around her shoulders and deep berry coloured lipstick she looked great, very different then how she looked when she was working at the Whistlestop. Clearly Ted was taking notice.

"It's nice to meet you, Nya." Ted shook her hand as

Cuddy smiled and waved. "Where are you ladies off to tonight?"

"Well, Camille has been telling me she can't cook. So I thought I would bring her by our place and teach her something," Millie said.

Cuddy laughed. "You got a fire extinguisher?"

"Yes. And I'm well insured," Millie replied with a wink.

I kissed Ted on the cheek. "Don't wait up."

"I won't, as long as you promise that I don't have to be a taste tester." He smiled and waved as we headed out.

Once we got outside, I said, "I hate lying to him."

"I know, but it's necessary," Millie replied as we got in her SUV.

"Where are we going?" I asked as we got moving.

"Another poker game. This one is not nearly as civilized. Be prepared. Things could get a little fucky," Nya said with a laugh.

"What's with the poker games? It seems like there are a lot of them."

"There are. It's how people trade things and information. Where we are going is not as pleasant as Madam Vo's," Millie began. "There is a pair of gloves for you on the back seat, Camille."

"Awesome. Thank you. I was going to grab some and totally forgot." I looked around for them on the seats and found them on the black floor mat. They must have fallen when I got in. Luckily, they stretched over top of my mother's ring and up into my sleeve so I didn't have to worry about my wrists.

"Now, what do you mean by 'not as pleasant'? There are a lot of words I would use to describe yesterday, and none of them involve 'pleasant'." I asked.

Millie chuckled. "Do you know anything about the neighbourhood just east of downtown? Within walking distance of the Eaton Centre?"

The Eaton Centre was a large shopping mall in the middle of downtown Toronto. Lots of things surrounded it, including the campus of Ryerson University. Just east of it was a dangerous area filled with drug dealers, hookers, gangs, and every other ingredient you would need to make a cesspool. Where Chinatown was a mix of lights and sounds, this neighbourhood was verging on being a slum. Dark and dirty, the air smelt like sweat and filth. I became very conscious of how dark it was, and that we were surrounded by shadows.

"Fun fact, the brothel Jesse was running is in that neighbourhood. He frequented the area, so I know a little." Why I was so chipper about such a terrible fact, I couldn't tell you.

"Well, Burnt Offerings is a dangerous place where all the bottom of the barrel hang out. I got word Lilly Darling *might* be there," Millie said.

"*Might?* She would not set foot in Burnt Offerings!" Nya snapped.

"Did you forget she is hiding? Burnt Offerings is *exactly* where she would be."

The sign for the bar was literally a piece of burnt wood. Nailed above the doorway like someone would nail a cross, the piece of charred log had no words or identifiers. I assumed that whoever came here knew exactly where they were going. They wouldn't spend too much time wandering the street looking for a name above the doorway. With darkened windows, the place hummed with activity like an angry beehive.

"Are you ready, Camille?" Millie asked.

I smiled, sliding my gloved hands in my pockets. "Absolutely."

Millie motioned for us to follow her, and I felt something wash over us, like Millie's protective energy had formed a ball around us. She had never told me anything about the nature of her powers. I had no clue what she, or Nya for that matter, were capable of.

Burnt Offerings was very busy and smelled like cigarettes, even though smoking had been banned in bars and restaurants in Toronto for some time. Perhaps it was something they pumped out to add to the atmosphere. You could not have a bar with 'burnt' in the name and not have it smell like smoke at least a little.

The lights were dimmed, so it was hard to see people, but I tried to observe as much as I could as we moved through the clusters of people towards the back. A large bar seemed to take up an entire wall, with various sizes of tables near the front. As it had been at Madam Vo's, there was a door at the back of the room; this one off to the side of a small stage. Sitting on a stool near the stage was a very large man watching the crowd.

Millie approached him with a big smile. "Evening, Skip.

How's the weather today?"

Skip turned and smiled at us, his eyes blinking horizontally then vertically like he had two sets of eyelids. His eyes appeared to be black, with no discernible pupil or iris. It may have been because of how dark it was in the room or their natural colour. It was hard not to stare, but I was curious.

"Evening, Millie. What's a pretty girl like you doing in a shithole like this?" he asked.

"You know I come here for the ambiance, Skip. You remember my daughter, Nya. This is my niece, Camille."

He smiled at us, and then went and opened the door. He would have had to duck to enter, but once he had it open he sat back down on his stool. It was impressive that the stool supported his weight he was that huge.

It was black beyond the doorway; so thick and solid I could reach out and touch it. I suddenly got very nervous, and an acidic taste bubbled up from my throat and into my mouth. Like walking through *that* was my true entrance into this insanity. Once I went through *that* door, there was no turning back.

Nya leaned towards me. "The night is dark and full of terrors."

"Did you just quote *Game of Thrones*?"

"Seemed appropriate in this context." Her eyes went from the door to me. "You get that whatever comes up, we can handle it. Right?"

"It's not that. I'm used to anticipating what sort of situation I'm walking into. Being able to plan for every possible scenario I can imagine. Always being prepared for anything, often one step ahead of the situation." I took a calming breath. "I can't do that anymore. That will take time for me to get used to."

"That's understandable. But you're not alone. We are here, and we're not going anywhere."

"Another thing I have to get used to. None of you were ever part of my life."

Nya linked arms with mine. "I am sorry for that. But we are here now. So let's go get your friend back. Hopefully we'll find the traitor while we're at it."

The three of us walked through that dark ominous doorway. Nothing happened, except us entering a dark hallway. Nothing changed.

There was a bunch of noise and voices and the clinking of glasses along with some clouds of smoke.

As we walked down the hallway, I tried to walk tall, confident, and strong. I kept my arm linked with Nya but concealed my gloved hands as much as possible. So far, I had three plausible explanations of why I was wearing the gloves, including being a germophobe, skin disorders, and a condition called Raynaud's syndrome. Hopefully it wasn't something anyone noticed.

The room had wall sconces with old fashioned light bulbs that glowed an odd yellowy colour, with small tables and a bar at the back. There were more people here than there had been at Madam Vo's; much more black leather and beards, like something out of a biker bar.

Lots of heads turned when we entered, most only glanced at us though. I caught a glimpse of Liam Fitzpatrick at one of the tables and smiled. He smiled back and nodded.

"You want a drink?" Nya asked as she pulled me to the bar.

The hair on the back of my neck stood up. The bartender was tall and thin and bald. I couldn't immediately tell whether they were male or female. Dressed in all black with a complexion to match, parts of exposed skin shimmered blue when whatever it was moved.

"Absolutely."

I tried my best to look cool as I slid onto a barstool, but I was sure I failed miserably.

Millie chuckled. "I am going to go mingle. You two stay out of trouble."

She headed across the room, trying to be subtle about moving towards Liam Fitzpatrick, but even she wasn't that slick. She turned a few heads as she went, some gazes lingering a little longer than others.

"Random question. Millie is single, right?" I said quietly to Nya.

She glanced at her mom. "Oh, you caught that too? It's cool. She's single."

"Another random question. Where is your dad?"

"Mount Pleasant Cemetery."

"Shit! I'm an asshole. Sorry, dude. I had no idea."

"We don't talk about it a whole lot. We're good. No worries."

"Can I ask what happened to him?"

"It's hard to explain. Do you know anything about elementals?"

"Like earth, fire, air, water type elements?"

"Yep. Those ones."

"Yeah, no. I wasn't kidding when I said I know fuck all about," I motioned around the room, "*all of this*."

"Long story short, he was killed by an elemental. One of the fire ones. I didn't see it happen, but Mom said it was quick."

"What happened to whoever did it?"

Nya chuckled. "My mom dealt with them. Pissing her off is a bad idea."

I studied Nya's face. "You seem so calm and casual about it all. Like its business as usual."

"I could say the same thing to you about what happened with Harold and his people. You'll come to understand when you have spent more time in this world. Shit like that happens, and you just go with the flow," she said.

People dying is the flow?

There was a ruckus on the other side of the room, and we both turned to see two big guys in a heated argument. Smoke seemed to swirl around them. One was taller with a very long beard. The other looked like he had no hair anywhere on his head, no eyebrows or eyelashes either.

Duck Dynasty versus Victor Zazz from Batman?

"Do you see the traitor anywhere?" I asked. "We've been sitting here chatting and totally got off topic."

Nya scanned the room, then held out her hand and stared at her palm. I leaned over and looked too. Whatever she was seeing, I couldn't.

"No. And she hasn't been here either, from what I can tell," Nya said, closing her hand and lowering it back by her leg.

The heated argument on the other side of the room was getting worse, and I jumped when one of the men flipped a table with the same ease that one would flip a playing card, sending it crashing to the ground where it exploded in pieces of wood.

It seemed like everyone in the room got up, and the yelling and smashing got louder. Nya and I headed for the closest wall to get out of the way. When I saw someone throw a punch, I knew we needed to go.

"Where's Millie?" I had to raise my voice to talk over the yelling. "We should go."

"I don't know. I don't see her." Nya held tightly to my wrist as she stood on her tip toes and tried to see into the crowd.

We attempted to move along the wall towards the door but didn't get far. The room was getting more and more volatile by the minute.

Millie finally appeared from within the chaos. "Time to go, girls."

We pushed our way through the throng of people towards the door. It seemed like everyone was involved in the scuffle, except us.

An impossibly large dude was punching a smaller

guy in front of the exit. It would take some serious manoeuvring to get around him.

"Fuck!" Millie cursed. She was about to push her way passed when someone grabbed my free wrist from behind us.

My breath caught in my throat when I came face to face with Eric. I had no words, no thoughts other than I am fucked with a capital F. The scenario's of exactly how bad this was going to be ran through my head like clips from an after school special.

I could bullshit my way through *a lot* but not this.

"This way!" he said.

"Who the hell are you?" Millie snapped. "You know this guy, Cas?"

"Yeah, he's Lewis's protégée." I didn't think my voice was loud enough for anyone to hear, but I was angry and pretty damn embarrassed.

"He's *what?*" Millie yelled.

"Calm down. I'm a Merlin. And unless you plan on vaulting over that fight, you need to come with me."

Millie nodded, and we turned and followed Eric. I hesitated at first but continued on with Nya and Millie. I had the overwhelming urge to run like hell. Run back to the safety of my bed and my teddy bear, because adding one more thing to this shit storm would make me explode.

"What the fuck is a Merlin?" I yelled as we pushed in the opposite direction of the exit. Another door appeared at the very back of the room. I hadn't noticed it when we came in.

"Are you ignoring me? What the *fuck* is a Merlin?" I continued to raise my voice as we pushed our way out the door, dumping us into an alley.

"Alright. Stop! We're not going anywhere until you explain!" I yelled at Eric, shaking free of his grip. Looking at his face, my fear turned to anger, and I went on the defensive. I wasn't about to blindly believe any shit that came out of his mouth.

He looked confused. "You really don't know?"

"Her mother had bound her powers and told her nothing. She only found out recently," Millie explained. She was so casual about it I was shocked.

"How did you find us?" I snapped. My insides were vibrating so hard I felt like I might sprout wings and take flight. So many emotions swirled through me I had trouble picking just one, and I didn't want him to see any of them.

"I followed you," he said.

"Why?"

"Because I knew something was going on, and you would need my help." He was so calm and collected, like I was just supposed to accept his reason. Like I wasn't going to prove the fuck out of his raspberry inducing answer.

"Is that why you got a job at L&B? Because you needed to *help me*?"

"No! Not at all. That was just a coincidence. Believe it or not, I actually enjoy the job." His expression was full of concern.

"Why should I believe you? And what the fuck is a Merlin? I thought Merlin was a dude?"

"Merlin is a title. An office. Kind of like the Dalai Lama," Nya chimed in. "They go through this picking item ritual and everything. It's cool. I will explain later."

"How the hell am I supposed to trust you? Do you really think I believe that it was just a coincidence that you got a job at L&B right around the time I find out I'm—" I could feel myself getting heated. I needed to calm down. Not the best time to expose my hand to the table.

Poker analogy? Get a life, lame-o.

He laughed. "That you're a le Fay? I think you're being a bit dramatic."

Pausing, I watched him for a few moments, studying him like I had at the office. Looking for clues, tells, anything that would give me a sense of if he was lying or not. And I got nothing.

Either he is a fantastic liar, or he has no clue what I am.

"But we can discuss that elsewhere. This is not the best place to be hanging out in a dark alley." He motioned for us to follow him, and we headed out to the street. Deciding to wait and not continue the interrogation was very hard, but necessary.

There was a group of people hovering ahead of us near the exit of the alley. I couldn't see their faces, but something seemed off. Their gait when they walked like their joints were broken and fixed wrong, and their head movements were more twisted and unnatural than a normal person. They looked like zombies shuffling along with no path in particular.

Eric wavered, eyeing the cluster of weirdness. Millie stopped when he did, her eyebrows rising.

The group shifted weirdly, and my body erupted in goose bumps. Their presence felt like a weight around my ankles, dragging me down into a cold darkness I did not understand. A shadowy aura loomed beside us, and as I reached out for it, it vanished.

I'd felt that shadow before and was never quite sure exactly what it was. That was another question to add to the 'let's talk about it later' list.

"We should go the other way," Millie said, and the group stopped. They all turned in unison and looked at us. Glowing eyes blinked like a bunch of raccoons. They made a strange skittering noise like the trash panda's did when they were scared.

"What the fuck are those?" I asked, pointing in their direction. I guess I spoke a little too loud because they started coming towards us. I could almost hear the click from when their bones shifted to move in a new direction.

Millie started backing up. "We should run."

"Why? Isn't this why we have powers?" I snapped. Nya had a firm grip on my wrist and pulled me along with them.

"We can't just slaughter people in the street," Millie said. "That's not how this works."

"Who said anything about slaughter? We just have to knock them down long enough to get away." I raised my hand to use my powers, and Eric grabbed it before I could.

He looked down quizzically at my gloves. "That's an odd fashion statement. But no, we just need to run."

He kept a grip on my hand as we fully turned and started running, only to find another group of twitchy weirdos coming in our direction.

"Shit," Millie grumbled.

"I think I know what those are." Eric kept his eyes on them. "They're vampires."

"They're *what?* I've never seen a vampire like that." I tried to hide my fear.

You haven't seen that many vampires, dummy.

"They're feral. They were food to a cabal, got turned, and malnourished. Not feeding does something to a vamp's brain. It's hard to explain. They're like meth heads," Eric said quietly to me, my hand firmly in his. I didn't even try to pull away from him.

"Can we do magic now?" I asked. The three of them looked at me like I was an idiot.

"Cas, don't forget, you can't—" Millie began.

"But I can do the easy stuff? The common stuff?" I asked.

"Why are you arguing over what she can and cannot do? Just do what you have to do to keep us alive." Eric raised his free hand, and as his lips moved a burst came from him, knocking several of them off their feet and sending them flying.

"Do we need to discuss the issues around using magic out in the open?" Nya asked.

"That depends. Do you feel like getting eaten? Because I sure don't," Eric replied. I went to raise my hands to use my powers, and my glove started to slip off into Eric's grip.

"Why do you have these things on anyhow?" Eric asked as he pulled the loose glove off the rest of the way. His eyes widened as he got a look at my white as snow extremity.

I snatched the glove from him and put it back on. He watched me, completely dumbfounded. I kept my eyes turned away from him. I didn't want him to see the panic in my eyes.

"Not the time or the place." He could not have faked that facial expression. I was happy to see that he genuinely had no clue what I was before that moment.

"*Not the time or the place. But the time to figure out how the fuck we're going to get out of here!*" Nya's panicked voice brought me back to reality, and I looked around at the crowd that had encircled us.

Their raccoon-eyed, sunken in faces were examining us like they wanted to feast on our brains. Bulbous eyeballs seemed to glimmer red in the streetlights. When they moved, there was a sickening crack, like their bones were breaking while they walked. That same skittering noise was louder now and made my skin crawl.

"Let me try something," I said quickly.

"*No*," Millie snapped.

"No one is watching. Besides, there are no guarantees it will work. But if it does, it's a game changer," I continued. "Don't worry about him. You trusted him enough to get us out. There is a file on him at work. If he starts acting up," I sarcastically whispered loud enough for him to hear, "we can hunt his ass."

I smiled a big-toothed grin at Eric before I closed my eyes. I focused in on the crowd around us, and a patch of darkness that I found within myself that seemed to connect to them.

That patch opened up inside me and spread out towards them, wrapping around each one like a cloud of smoke. It was different than my threads but just as consuming. They all seemed to stand up a little straighter, and collectively turn towards me.

"Now, I need one of you to take my arm and guide me out while I part them. Can you do that?" I asked.

"How the fuck are you doing that?" Nya said, very close beside me.

"Not sure. But are they calm? Is it okay for us to move?" I felt a hand grab my wrist. Not only did I feel calmer, but I got a power surge that freaked me out. Like a caffeine jolt, but crazier.

"Yeah, they're good." From what I could feel of this new energy, Eric was the one holding my hand.

"Okay. I'm going to part them now. I don't know how long this will hold, or what they will be like when I lose control. Be prepared."

We began to shuffle along. The things parted, and we were making our way through them when suddenly there was a loud snap. I jumped, opening my eyes as I lost my connection. We weren't quite through the crowd, and were very close to the edge of the alley.

One came at me, snapping its teeth like a rabid dog. I jumped back into Eric.

I stared the thing in the eyes and screamed as loud as I could. "No!"

My scream erupted like a shock wave, sending bodies flying like blowing leaves. Eric took that as an opening, and with one hand firmly around my wrist, we ran all the way back to Millie's SUV. We got in without another word and drove off.

"You got a vehicle somewhere?" Millie asked Eric after we had been on the road for a minute.

"No, I took public transit. Parking downtown is a bitch," he replied. "I'm Eric Sadler by the way. Sorry we had to meet like this. I wanted to introduce myself in a different way but—"

"But that's a weird conversation. 'Hey, you're a le Fay and I'm a Merlin. Whoopie.'" I tried not to sound too sarcastic. "It's cool. Thank you for saving our asses."

"I should be thanking you. What exactly did you just do back there?"

I felt myself blush. "I'm not sure. This is all pretty new to me."

"We'll figure it out, Cas. One thing at a time. First, we have to find Lilly Darling," Millie said. I looked at her face in the rear-view mirror. I could tell she was getting frustrated.

"Did you go to Madam Vo's?" Eric asked.

"Yep. Last night. They have no clue where she is."

"My guess is that she is hiding at The Matador."

Millie exhaled loudly. "Of course she is. Out of all the god forsaken places she had to go."

"What's The Matador?" I asked.

"I think we should all sit down and have a little chat. Eric, do you mind coming to my place? I will take you wherever you need once we're done." Millie said, her tone was stern enough that it was clear she was trying to be friendly but meant business.

Eric smiled and nodded. "Absolutely."

Millie lived in a little house by the lake that looked like a cottage. Red bricks and a slate roof gave it a rustic feel. The outside was well maintained, with what would have been a very lush garden in the warmer weather surrounding the outside. The backyard was probably beautiful. She clearly took great pride in her home.

Inside was much larger than it looked from the outside. The 1950s style bungalow had large windows that would let in a lot of light during the day. Dark hardwood floors ran throughout, with a mix of some antique furniture and clearly well-loved pieces. Millie directed us to the front room that had a large fireplace, leather couches, and a worn Persian rug. The dark blue paint on the walls gave the room a very soothing feeling.

"I will go make some tea," Millie said, and she and Nya fluttered out of the room, leaving Eric and I sitting on one of the couches.

"So, this is weird, right?" I said, and we both laughed. My cheeks flushed.

"Yeah. It's weird." He chuckled. "But I'm glad it happened. We needed to have this conversation. We should have after that first day with the...." He gestured awkwardly with his amazing, strong hand.

"The weird shock thing when we shook hands? That *was* strange."

"It was, and I didn't know how to bring it up. Even though tonight sucked, it answered a lot of questions."

I smiled. "So, you're a Merlin?"

"Yeah. The other candidates for the title are still around. They kind of work for me I guess. They're sort of like...."

"Disciples?"

"Yeah, kind of. They have similar powers, but there is no guarantee they will ever take my place. It's hard to explain. In a generation, there are seven or so candidates, and we go through a ritual to select the Merlin. The ones who are not chosen are trained by the one who is in a variety of ways. We're like brothers. I like having them around."

"Wow. Sounds like a lot of pressure."

He shrugged. "Sometimes. That's not even getting into being a deity to a certain group of druids."

"I thought being the prophecy girl was nuts."

"About that. I have some questions," he began. "Your parents were killed when you were young, right? That never brought out any of your powers?"

"No. My mother bound my powers. I have been told that it's a surprise that the spell held up after she died."

"If she used blood magic to bind you, no it's not a surprise. Given the circumstances, I am not surprised she bound you. So when your boyfriend—"

"He wasn't my boyfriend at the time. But my grandfather Harold LeFaye and his group killed Jesse to jump start my prophecy. I went to Harold's house under the ruse that his wife, my grandmother, was dying. She was, but he took it as an opportunity to unbind my powers."

"Wow, that's heavy."

"You have no idea. I did some things after that that I'm not proud of. But they won't bother me anymore."

He smiled and put his hand on my knee. I instantly felt better. "I wish I could say that would be the last time that will happen in your life. But as someone who has lived this life being one of the 'chosen' so to speak, I can't make any promises."

"Thank you for even thinking of it. I appreciate that."

"Why are you looking for Lilly Darling?" Eric asked. Millie and Nya reappeared with a tray of tea and cookies.

"My friend, Bliss, was kidnapped by the Kinkaid's."

"Okay. Why?"

"They think she knows something about what

happened to Lucia Kinkaid."

"*What happened to Lucia Kinkaid?*"

"Why does everyone keep saying that? I don't know! But they think my friend knows something so they kidnapped her. When Tobias Kinkaid decided to claim her during this process, I have no idea. But I knew he had a thing for Bliss beforehand, maybe he figured this was a good time to act on it."

"And you need Lilly Darling because?"

Millie answered Eric as she handed us our mugs of tea. "Lilly works for the Kinkaid's. She will know how to find Bliss."

"We were told she ghosted because she had a premonition about the *rise* of *Blanchmains*," I said, and he raised his eyebrows.

"Oh. So it's not common knowledge?" he asked.

"Absolutely not. And we will be keeping it that way," Millie said, giving him a look that could have cut him in half. I hid my smile behind my tea cup.

He raised his hands in defeat. "Your secret is safe with me. Like Camille said, she has a file on me at the office. I am legit. I just want to be friends."

"I believe you," Nya said, grinning as she twisted a strand of hair around her finger.

I wondered in that moment if he was actually good looking or if this was part of his magic. Or if it was just the fact that he looked an awful lot like a certain crossbow wielding zombie hunter. He turned his eyes to me and something inside me responded. Whatever it was, I liked him. I couldn't deny it.

We talked a little while longer. I noticed Millie relax and grow more comfortable as time went on, and I knew then that he was okay. Eric was charming and friendly, and I caught Nya batting her eyelashes a few times.

After I yawned more than once, we all deemed it was time to wrap it up and head home. We made a plan to go to The Matador the next night.

When I finally got home and was drifting off to sleep, my phone beeped.

It was a text from an unknown number, but I knew immediately it was Eric.

Really happy everything is out in the open now. See you in the morning.

5.

I rode with Ted to the office in the morning. By the time we got there, I was on my third cup of coffee. With coming back late and not much sleep, I needed to caffeinate. I wasn't used to having such an active social life.

I sat in my office and stared at my computer for a while. I had no idea what we were walking into tonight, not just in dealing with The Matador, but also Lilly Darling. I was new to this world when everyone else wasn't, so I thought I should educate myself the only way I knew how. Staring at my computer like an idiot didn't help at all.

It was time for me to vet Lilly Darling and do some digging into The Matador.

Lilly had an active social media presence that stopped around the time Bliss went missing. Premonition implied seeing something happen before the actual event, so I had no clue how long she had been gone for.

Maybe she got premonition confused with vision.

Lilly was cute. Small. She easily could have passed for thirteen years old, and she was ten years older, according to her Facebook profile. With long black hair and big blue eyes, she had an elfish quality. She was so pale she almost glowed like she had a candle lit somewhere inside her.

She had a lot of friends on Facebook and followers on Twitter and Instagram. There were no signs of magic. No mention of Peter Pan or anything. Not that I expected her to have, like, a detailed blog about her life or a YouTube confessional. Frankly, after what had happened with Jane Lowry, I didn't know what to expect.

I read a little into Peter Pan. There was a lot about the fiction and nothing that could even be considered logically plausible. Trying to piece together what, if any of it, was truthful would take more time than I had at the moment. But I was curious. Maybe she would tell me one day.

The Matador was down a small side street in Little Italy and had been in business for decades. It was originally a salsa club and dance hall, and when that went out of fashion, it became a venue that hosted a variety of different types of events, ranging from wedding receptions to christenings to wakes.

That was what was public record. A quick peek at their financials showed they weren't hurting for business. They were booked solid every Friday and Saturday night for the foreseeable future, with the only explanation on their online calendar being 'booked for an owner's event'. Trying to find the name of the current owner was a totally different story.

While I was digging, there was a knock at my door. I was so zoned out, I had totally forgotten that I was at work. I probably had clients today.

"Come in!" I called out, smoothing my hair and lightly slapping my cheeks to try to wake myself up, hoping a little colour made me look less tired.

The door opened a crack, and Eric stuck his head in. "Good morning."

"Hey," I said, breathing a sigh of relief. "I was just doing some digging on Lilly Darling and The Matador."

He came into my office, holding two coffee mugs, and closed the door behind him with his elbow.

He handed me a mug across the desk and said, "You didn't have to do that. I would have told you...wait, never mind. I would have done my own digging too. What do you want to know? Maybe I can help you."

"You've got to understand, this is all new to me. *All of it*. I don't deal well walking into situations that I don't have a plan A through K for. Especially without my people."

"Millie and Nya?"

"*Millie and Nya are my mom's people.* That's the major part about all of this. I may be the 'prophecy girl' and whatever, but I don't feel like I am one of *them*." I examined his expression. "I'm sorry, I don't want to pile my shit on you."

"It's cool. I get it. I can't imagine what all this is like for you. I was raised knowing exactly what this world is, and what I am. My mother always believed that I was *the* Merlin."

My eyes lowered. "I wish I could talk to my mom."

"Has no one talked to you about that?"

"Not really."

"Well, *we* will. Soon, I promise. But one thing at a time."

"Fine. Now, what can *you* tell me about Lilly Darling?"

"I don't follow."

"You do know her, don't you? Or did I read that wrong? You had a lot of suggestions of where she could be. The likely explanation, considering you wouldn't know where she would be if you only vetted her, is that *you know her*. So, what can you tell me about Lilly Darling?"

His face remained expressionless for a few minutes as we stared at one another, like two dogs watching each other, waiting to see if the other would advance.

"Anyone ever tell you you're good at this?"

"It's my Spidey sense. Stop trying to distract me."

"She dated one of the others for a bit."

"Your disciples?"

"I hate that word, but yes. I believe she thought he would be number two and broke up with him when he wasn't."

"That's kind of sad."

He shrugged. "Some call her a traitor. I call her an opportunist. If she sees a way to advance herself and her cause, she will take it. And he is very naive when it comes to women. Girls like Lilly chew threw him on a regular basis."

"Her 'cause'?"

"Lilly is big on trying to prove that her Pan claim is not only legitimate but real. She has powers, I have seen them. But the idea that they are one of the noble magical families...lots of people aren't going for it. Hooking herself up with the Kinkaid's is just another way for her to, in her mind, prove her point."

"Do her powers involve premonitions or visions? We were told she had one about the rise of *Blanchmains* and that's why she ghosted."

"I don't know. But you may hear stories like that from a lot of people. It's a bit of a thing, *the rise of Blanchmains*, as you call it."

I blushed, and before I could ask questions, there was a knock at my door.

"Right! We're at work!" He jumped up, grabbed his coffee, and headed for the door. I was surprised, when he opened it, to find Q and Lemme with large Frappuccino's in hand, including one for me.

"Shit! Hi, guys! This is Eric, Lewis's new protégée. Eric, this is Q and Lemme." I stood up and smiled, motioning for them to come in. "They're tech support... among other things."

"Nice to meet you both. Camille, we'll talk more later." He smiled and winked at me as he walked out the door.

"Holy shitballs, dude! Do you know who he looks like?"

Q said as she came in. She was grinning ear to ear, her long black hair was half braided back in cornrows and the other half hung loose past her shoulders. She was wearing a green Adidas tracksuit and white sneakers.

"Yeah, I know who he looks like," I replied, sitting back down.

"Are you into that? Because if you're not, I am totally down. Just give me ten minutes." Q stared at my door like she was ready to run out and pounce on Eric.

"Fuck! I totally forgot!" I grabbed my purse and dug around for the kit Lemme had given me. I found the samples Bliss and I had taken from Lucia Kinkaid and handed them to her.

"Another one?" Lemme asked.

"Possibly a…what's the word…host?"

Lemme smiled happily. "Cool. Thanks, brah."

Q finally turned her attention to me. "So, what's his deal?"

I laughed. "Not a clue. I have only talked to him a handful of times. But if Lewis is bringing him in, he must be solid."

"True. Maybe we will cruise by his office when we are done. You got that phone for me?" Q asked.

I handed her Jesse's phone out of my bag. "You can't leave the building with it, Q. My cousin said her higher ups are bugging out. If it's not here when she comes to get it, she'll probably write us all up for obstruction or withholding or some shit."

"No problemo." Q put down her drink and pulled

her laptop out of her bag. She snapped off the back of Jesse's phone. Using her own phone, she took a photo of it and Jesse's SIM card before plugging his phone into her laptop.

"So, what's on the docket right now?" Lemme asked. Her dark brown hair was piled high in a bun on top of her head. Judging from its overall size, I would say her hair was almost to her waist. I envied them both with their long dark luxurious locks.

"Nothing at the moment. I don't think, anyways." I reached over and took a sip of my Frappuccino. "I am not fully awake yet."

"You feeling alright?"

"Yeah, just not sleeping so well."

Q chuckled. "You know what helps me sleep? Smoking a bowl before bed."

"Pot makes me paranoid, dude," I replied.

"Me too. That shit does not solve everyone's problems, dummy." Lemme punched Q in the shoulder lightly. The silver rings she had on each finger sparkled, looking an awful lot like not-brass brass knuckles.

"You just don't have the right shit, I'm telling you." Something beeped, and Q unplugged Jesse's phone from her laptop and handed it back to me. "I will let you know if I find anything worthwhile, Bond. How are you dealing with all of this?"

"All of what?" I asked, taking another sip of my drink. As they both stared at me a little dumbfounded, I noticed that they were in coordinating tracksuits, only Lemme's was blue.

"Dude. You don't have to do that. Jesse went from just being dead to possibly murdered. It's okay if you're not dealing."

I rolled my eyes. "Why do people assume that? I'm good. Maybe it's wrong that I'm good, but I am. When you're involved with a junkie, death is always on the table. I know it sounds a little fucky, but I was kind of prepared."

"Alright. I get it. How are things with your rock star?" Q asked.

"Not a clue. He's been a ghost for a few days. I'm going to call him."

"Well, we'll leave you to it," she said, and they packed up their stuff.

"Thanks for the caffeine, by the way." I said as they were walking out the door.

"Anytime. We'll let you know if we find anything."

As soon as my door closed, I picked up my phone and called Fray. I hadn't spoken to him in a few days, and I wanted to hear his voice.

The phone rang a bunch of times, then someone finally picked up.

"Hello?" The female voice was surprisingly chipper. My heart began to feel like a beating mass of dead weight, and I had a flash of who I had thought was a girl that Fray was sneaking out of his apartment the last time I was there.

Not this shit again.

"Hi," I chippered right back, because why the fuck not. "Who is this?"

"I'm Nikki. Who is this?"

"Hi, Nikki. I'm Camille. I'm looking for Fray. This is the right number, isn't it?"

"Oh hey, Camille! Fray told me a lot about you. Hang on one sec." She covered the receiver with her hand, and there was some shuffling. Then silence. A wave of rage crashed into me, and I had to bite back a scream. He spoke about me to this woman? What the hell was happening?

Finally, after a few minutes, he said, "Hello?"

"Hey! It's Camille. How are you?" I tried my best to keep up the chipper voice and hide my anger. Because, in reality, I knew better than to ever think that Noah Fray would *only* want to be with me.

"I'm okay, how are you?"

"Good!"

He was silent for a few moments before saying, "Listen, I think I should explain..."

"No need to explain! You made no commitments to me. And please don't think I was silly enough to believe all that schmooze talk." I chuckled awkwardly. "I mean, you can *literally* have any girl you want. Why would you ever choose someone like me?"

"Cas—"

I bit back my tears and tried to keep my tone friendly. "Hey, have you heard from Bliss at all? I can't find her, and I'm worried."

He managed to stutter out, "N–no–no, I haven't. Sorry. Did you track her phone?"

My Spidey sense started tingling. I couldn't tell if I was wigged out by 'Nikki' or if there was something fishy going on. I didn't understand how the Spidey sense worked, but I knew enough to pay attention when it was warning me about something. Or someone.

"Okay. Well, if you speak to her, can you tell her to call me? I would really appreciate it."

"I will. Can I come—"

"Sorry, I have to get back to work. I don't have time right now."

"How about tonight?"

I paused, and the chipperness wore off. "No, I think I'm good. Tell Bliss to call me. Beyond that, I think we're done. No need to trouble yourself with trying to explain."

I turned off my phone and put it on my desk. I breathed deeply a few times to try to calm my nerves.

Maybe I overreacted. Maybe there was a perfectly innocent explanation. She was his assistant. Or worked for his record label. Or his maid.

Or I am the biggest schmuck around.

I stayed in my office until I finished both coffees, and then decided to go looking for food. The caffeine jitters were a little disconcerting but focusing on them stopped me from focusing on other bullshit, so it worked out.

Leaving the safety of my office made me feel like someone had popped my bubble. The emotions I had been pushing back came crashing into me like a wave.

I wanted to cry and scream all at the same time. Why me?

I wandered into the breakroom and found a plate of pastries. I randomly grabbed one and felt a hand on my back as I stuffed it in my face.

"That was the infamous Q, huh?" Eric smiled happily until I turned around, then his eyes widened.

"Uh, Camille. Are you okay?" he asked.

I shook my head no.

"Do you have your gloves?"

I looked down at my hands, and I shook my head again. In that moment, I didn't care who saw my white hands.

He wrapped his hands around mine, and all I could think about was how warm he was. I closed my eyes, and a tear rolled down my cheek. He took the pastry out of my mouth and put it on the table.

"What's going on?" he asked quietly.

"I must have 'gullible moron' tattooed somewhere that only dudes can see," I said.

"Maybe it's time to stop dealing with dudes and find a man." He said it so smoothly I was shocked.

I chuckled. "That was pretty slick, I'm impressed."

"You liked that? I'm happy I could make you smile."

"Thank you. To be honest, I'm not sure any man would be interested in a broken toy like me," I said.

He took his hands off mine, and I almost reached out for him; I didn't want him to let me go. But my hands had gone back to a normal colour.

He smiled at me, and I wanted to melt. "And who exactly are you, prophecy girl?"

"I don't know anymore."

He pushed a stray hair back from my face. We just stood and stared at each other in silence.

If anyone saw us, they would probably be deeply confused.

"Do you want your scone?" Eric asked me, ending our stare down.

I looked at him, then down at the pastry on the table. "Scone? Out of all the ones I grab, it's a damn scone?"

He picked it up and examined it. "It looks like chocolate chip."

"But a scone? Q must have spiked that Frappuccino with something."

"Yes, back to Q. Interesting girl. I've heard the legend from Ted and Chris, but maybe you can explain why she called me Daddy Daryl on her way out."

I covered my mouth to try to contain my laughter. Q wasn't playing when she said she would hit on Eric. I was just surprised by her aggressiveness.

"I'm glad you find it funny, because it kind of scared me," he said, and then he shook a little.

He got a little closer to me, and I was able to smell him; warm and woodsy with a hint of spice, and cinnamon.

I fucking love cinnamon.

He handed me the scone. "We should get back to work?"

"Should we? We could stay here a little longer. We could…." I got a little closer to him, and our eyes met, but then I stepped back. "You're right. We should go back to work. We'll talk more tonight, okay?"

He smirked, and I saw a little glimmer in his eyes. "Absolutely. Do you want me to pick you up?"

I turned and started walking away, calling over my shoulder, "Sure. I will let Millie know."

The rest of the day was a complete blur. Luckily, I had no clients. Not that I would have minded, but I was just not in the mindset at the moment.

I did some more digging on The Matador, and I found some interesting historical stuff that I thought we could discuss on the ride tonight. Not a lot of information about what was going on currently, but I was sure we could piece things together.

Goddamn I'm a nerd.

I went home, showered, and was picking out some clothes when my phone rang. I picked it up without checking the call display.

"Hello?" I said happily, waiting for Eric's voice.

"Cas," I was genuinely shocked to hear Fray. "Cas, please don't hang up."

I chuckled. "Hang up? Why would I hang up?"

"I thought after what happened earlier with Nikki—"

"What happened earlier with Nikki?" he said nothing, so I continued. "Oh, hey, no. It's like I said before, you made no commitment to me. You have nothing to explain."

"But I—"

"But what? I am not going to sleep with you, Noah. If this was some elaborate ruse to get me to do that, you can stop now."

He laughed. "Is that all you think of me? Did you forget I am a rock star now? I can literally have any girl I want. I don't have to chase anyone."

"Truthfully? I think I'm a conquest. The one that got away. Once you have what you want, you won't want to bother with the real me." Whether anyone would want to bother with the real me was under question at the moment.

He laughed again, and before he could speak, I said, "Where the fuck is Bliss, Noah?"

He stopped laughing really fast. "Why would you think I know where she is? I only found out she went missing when you told me. That's why I'm calling. So I can *explain* what happened today, and so we can make a plan to look for Bliss. She's my friend, too, you know."

I laughed. I couldn't help it. Maybe I was nit picking, but I realized in that moment that my Spidey sense wasn't tingling because of Nikki.

"I never said she was missing. I just said I hadn't heard from her in a few days." My voice was flat and monotone.

"Whatever, you know what I meant. I assumed, okay? I didn't think you would play that kind of game with me. I thought we had something real, Cas. When we were lying on my floor I thought we had a moment. Are you going to try to tell me now that we didn't?"

"Who's Nikki?"

Silence. Which was what I expected. Part of me knew that Noah was a good person. Honest. Real. But another part of me knew Fray—the rock star who could fuck any girl he wanted—wouldn't go to so much trouble for no reason. For someone who could literally have any girl they wanted to put that much effort in...

Did I want to dissect it further? If I pushed the issue then I could end up stuck with him, and I wasn't sure I wanted that.

"She helped us get our deal. She's just a friend. That's all. You can meet her. You'll like her."

Jesse said that, too, once. About a girl who was broken, like him. He thought I could help her, like I had done for him so many times. He only made that mistake once, and never about the slut in white denim. Amanda. Whatever the fuck her name is. Maybe now I should call her the plague monkey. STD's combined with supervamp virus equals?

"Maybe one day. Look, I have to work tonight. We can talk more tomorrow," I tried to sound forceful so the conversation would end.

"Have dinner with me. I promise I will explain everything."

"I will call you tomorrow," I hung up without agreeing to anything. I had no reason to and did not intend to at any point.

I put on tight black pants, a black empire waist tank top that hung loose around my hips, and my usual boots. Then I did my hair and put on a little makeup. I thought I looked okay, but I didn't look at myself in the mirror long enough to dwell on it. If I did, I would never leave the house.

I put all my going out gear in my smaller purse, making sure it was easy for me to carry. If we ran into another problem like we did at Burnt Offerings, I didn't want my bag to be an issue.

When I got downstairs, there was a note from Ted saying he had a stakeout, and Cuddy and Poppy were nowhere to be found. So, I had a little something to eat while I waited for Eric.

I sat at the kitchen table and ate a sandwich, staring at my marble white hands. I had to find a way to keep calm. If my emotions were that tied to my powers, I would need to learn to control them or I would give myself away. I had my gloves, but unless I wanted to pretend that I was a germophobe, someone would catch on eventually.

A new le Fay with gloves on? Yep that's not suspicious.

My phone finally beeped, and it was Eric. I breathed a sigh of relief. He could help me get this situation with my hands under control.

That would also give me an excuse to hold his hand again.

Fuck, I needed help.

"This is not what I expected," I said when I got into Eric's four door black VW.

"Is that bad? Do you not want to ride with me?" he asked.

"No, I do! I do! I was just expecting...."

"What? A motorcycle? I wasn't sure you would get on one."

I shrugged. "Good point. So, do you want to hear about what I found?"

"Do you want to tell me about why your hands are white first or after?"

I looked down at my hands, trying to play dumb. "Oh, that? Just more stupid boy shit. It's a long story."

"You got your gloves?" I pulled them out of my purse and waved them at him. "Good. That is *not* a conversation we need to have in The Matador."

"Do you want to know what I found out about The Matador?" I asked as I put on the gloves.

"Absolutely."

"Well, it was originally created by a family called the Castillo's. They bought the building, remodelled it, and ran it as a supper club in the 40s. Then it seems it was a speakeasy, and many other things over the past X amount of years, but that is not the important part. What *is* important is that there is no evidence that it has changed owners. So, either it has been handed down in the Castillo family, or the original owner is still around."

"Which is still possible. They have only owned it for

seventy-eight years."

I smiled. "And if the original owner bought it when he was twenty *that would make him ninety-eight years old*."

He shrugged his shoulders. "That is interesting, and worth looking into. Maybe at the office when we're supposed to be working?"

"Or another time? I live with Ted still, but you could always come by? Or I could come to where you live?"

He glanced at me briefly, being careful to keep his eyes on the road. I already felt like an idiot. He hadn't responded, but he also didn't immediately shoot me down.

"Or not?" I felt my face turn red. "What should I expect when we get there?"

"Have you ever seen the movie *From Dusk Till Dawn*?"

"Are you serious?"

"I wish I wasn't."

He started parallel parking, and I looked outside the window. We were on a normal looking residential street.

"I don't understand," I said.

He got out of the car and came around and opened my door. He took my hand as I got out and pulled me into his arms.

"And for the record, anytime, anywhere," he said, and we stared into each other's eyes.

I smiled, and he let me go.

"I parked a few blocks away. It's cheaper and safer." He motioned for me to follow him, and we walked down the street.

The Matador was an older looking building with a white sign that went vertically up the side, the name in black block letters. It had still maintained its 1940's feel with its colour scheme and overall aesthetic. A larger dude sat on a stool by the front door, protected by a small awning overhead. Millie and Nya stood a few feet away from him.

They smiled happily when they saw us.

Seems they are warming up to Eric quite nicely.

"How are you feeling, Camille?" Millie asked as she and Nya embraced me.

"I'm okay. Happy that you guys are here. Not sure what to expect," I replied.

Nya smiled. "Oh, it would be wise to walk in with an open mind. This place is a little off the wall."

"Great," I said with as much sarcasm I could muster, which in that moment wasn't much. Nervousness was currently tossing my other emotions around like a baseball player throwing in from the outfield.

Inside was dark, like you would expect a bar to be, with lots of tables around and people drinking. It was bigger than it looked from the outside and had a stage at the far back with a group of belly dancers performing on it. One had a large snake around her neck as a decoration. There was something hypnotic about the snake dancer's eyes, they glowed a greenish acidy yellow that immediately made me think of something poisonous. But she was beautiful, her long hair was draped around her like a sheet, and her lips were such a bright cheery red they looked candy apple coated.

I grabbed onto Nya's sleeve as we weaved our way through the crowd towards the rear. Millie had seen something at the bar, and she immediately started towards it. She was so laser focused, she weaved through the people and the tables like a mouse running a maze to get food at the end.

In the very back corner, at the end of the bar, was a large booth with a round table where another poker game was going on.

But that wasn't what we were headed towards.

I only caught a glimpse of the person at the far corner of the bar, close to the wall. When I looked, it was like they phased in and out. I got a flash of the person, and then they were gone, but sometimes she would go fuzzy like they were part of a blurry digital photo or badly recorded video.

"A cloaking spell? Really?" Nya laughed.

Millie moved quickly and with purpose, reaching across the bar and grabbing the person by the arm and yanking her off her stool.

The flashing stopped.

The girl looked down at her arm, then her big blue eyes turned to us. They widened a bit when she saw me.

"Hello, Lilly," Millie said. "We need to talk."

6.

Millie pulled Lilly by the arm to a small, deserted booth in an empty corner of the club. We followed along, piling in around Lilly. I pushed in to make sure I was right beside her, and she slid away to try to get closer to Millie.

"What are you doing here, Lilly?" Millie probed the girl.

"Getting drunk. What are you doing here?" Lilly mumbled.

"Looking for you. We need some help."

"I can't help you. I am not equipped to help you. I can't do anything. Turns out everyone was right!"

Nya snorted. "Feeling sorry for yourself, traitor?"

"You have no idea, little girl. You have no fucking idea." Lilly stared at the table.

"Tell me about the virus, Lilly." Millie pulled on Lilly's arm to bring her back to reality.

"What about it? You got it? Here," she reached in her

purse and handed Millie a bunch of vials. "Cure it. Then be more fucking careful."

"What is the point of it? What are they doing? How do we make the cure?"

Lilly rolled her eyes. "You know, the stupid part is that if those fucking morons hadn't shown up, all of this could have been avoided. If Nikki hadn't found some idiots to find that last ingredient, it never would have happened. You can blame that stupid band." She turned and looked at me. "The local one. You know the name. You probably think the lead singer is hot."

I swallowed hard. Oh. God. "Obsidian Butterfly?"

"Yes! Those idiots brought Frankenstein his last ingredient, and then he created the virus. Fucking idiots. All of this to save their drummer to keep their deal."

"Can you help me find my friend?" I asked her, trying to fight back tears. My first interrogation, and I already wanted to cry. And puke too. This shit, about the band, could not be real.

Grow a pair or go home.

"Who's your friend?" she asked.

"Bliss Fiori."

She laughed. "You mean Tobias's new pet? I can tell you where she is, but she's gone. You can't save her. You can't save anyone from them. No one can. And it's my fault."

She looked at me and examined my face. I saw a little glimmer in her eye, and she smiled. The tension in her body seemed to ease, and she took a calming breath in and out.

"Or maybe you can." She slid closer to me, like a happy cat wanting to be petted. "I knew you would come. Maybe if I help you, it will help my karma for all the shit I did for them."

She grabbed a cocktail napkin and wrote something down, stuffing it into Millie's hand when she was finished.

"Here. This is the cure." She took one of the vials from Millie and put it in my hand. "Drink this now."

I took the cap off and drank the vial without a second thought. Another thing to add to the list of dumb shit I probably should have thought through a little more.

"You will need the blood of the truest believer," Lilly said. Millie nodded; she seemed to know what she meant. I had so many questions I didn't even know where to begin. Lilly rubbed her hand on her chin, deep in thought, then turned to me again. Her blue eyes were full of sadness and a deep, overwhelming aura of the lost.

"I wish I had chosen a different path. All I wanted was to be taken seriously in *this* world. They told me they would make me powerful, that my family could align with them and really be something. Do you have any idea what it's like to have to claw your way up from the bottom? To have to prove yourself at every turn?" She chuckled, looking away for a moment. "No, of course you wouldn't. You've been charmed since the beginning, people will only bow to you. I thought the Kinkaid's respected me and took me seriously, took my family name seriously. But they just turned me into a henchman, and I can't accept the person I have become. I can't deal with this." She grabbed my gloved hand and squeezed. "Save us. You can. You and him, together, can save us all."

My eyes welled up with tears. "I don't think I can. I only found out a few days ago."

"But you can. *And you will.* I have seen it." She laughed a little, then pulled another vial out of her purse.

"I have to find my friend. I have to help her."

"She can't be helped. Tobias Kinkaid is in love with her. She has been claimed. I am so sorry."

I was going to say more, but she drank her vial, leaned her head back, and closed her eyes.

"Do I need to take more than one vial? Am I safe?" I asked her.

She didn't reply. She stayed perfectly still with her head back and eyes closed.

"What the fuck?" Nya snapped, banging her palm flat on the table. "Hello? This is no time to take a nap, you dumb bitch! Wake the fuck up!"

That darkness inside me that had connected with those things outside Burnt Offerings began to vibrate like a cell phone on silent. I reached out to Lilly. A thread came out of my hand, it felt weaker than the others had as it slithered along towards her. It withered and faded away while trying to connect to her.

"I don't get it. Something is wrong," I said. "Could that be part of her cover spell?"

The three of them were silent as I stared at their

blank faces. I tried to reach out another of my threads to connect with her, but the same thing happened. I searched inside myself for that ball of energy and tried to mould it to grab onto Lilly. It reached out, feeling everyone else around us, but Lilly just wasn't there. I knew she had strong magic, but I figured *Blanchmains* could connect with her somehow. But nothing happened.

She just sat there. Did she not feel me trying to use my magic? Would that not be enough to make her react?

It took longer than it should have for me to realize she was dead.

"No! No! NO!" I screamed in her face. "You get back here, you bitch! I have to help my friend! What good are these stupid powers if *I can't help Bliss?*"

Eric reached out and grabbed my hand. Millie made her mothering face from across the table. I extended my hand out to try to physically grab Lilly's shirt when Eric grabbed that one too.

"You think I am joking? I will drag her dead body out of here and beat her senseless until she fucking comes back!" I yelled. "How do I put her whatever the fuck you call it back in her body? Her essence? Her soul? I can do that, right? I did it before."

"Cas." Millie said my name in that calm, parental tone that only pissed adults off.

"Oh, don't 'Cas' me. This is bullshit, and you know it. What good is any of this if you can't do anything when bad shit happens? Can I summon her? I am going to summon her then banish her to whatever hell the fuckin—"

Eric pulled me out of the booth. "We need to go. Now."

"Hell no! I am not going anywhere without...." I couldn't hear my own voice over the noise in the room as he pulled me back through the crowd and outside to the street.

"This is not happening. This is not fucking happening." I paced back and forth on the sidewalk. I was at the end of my rope and was about to lose my shit. My anger, along with my magic, pulsed inside me, and my hands began to throb. I started shaking my hands beside me as if I was shaking off water, trying to help lessen the pulsing pain that was working its way up to my elbows.

"We can work with the info she gave us," he told me. "It's not over. We can still find her."

Nya and Millie came out a little while after. Their expressions were grim.

"We told the bartender. They're going to deal with the body," Millie said when she got close to us. "I am so sorry, Camille."

"This seems so wrong! She just kills herself like that, and no one calls the cops? This is so wrong!" I exclaimed. At that point I didn't care who heard me.

"They will deal with it, and her family will be notified." She showed me the napkin with writing on it. "But we have the cure. And you have taken it."

"We should be able to figure out exactly what it's made of from the vials she gave us. Unless she left an ingredient out," Nya added. "What is this shit about a band? What the fuck is she talking about?"

"I was more concerned about her saying *Frankenstein*," Millie mumbled.

"Should I just get used to the pile of bodies around me? With the stupid—" I went to take off my gloves, and Nya reached out and grabbed me, pulling me close to her. She was stronger than she looked.

"I get that you're mad. I would be mad too. But what you are about to do will only make this all a hundred times worse, I promise. I know it's hard when you're angry, but you have to think before you act," she said quietly to me, then turned to her mother. "Seems the temper is genetic."

Millie laughed. "You probably don't remember Marie, Nya. But her temper was legendary. Why do you think Cas didn't know about us? Because Harold pissed Marie off, and she disowned the entire family line."

That caused me to stop. "I have no memory of my mother ever getting angry."

"That was probably because her parents were out of the picture."

Eric stared at me with the strangest look on his face, and it was starting to freak me out. As if he was trying to recall a memory that was buried far back in his mind.

"Marie le Fay was your mom?" he asked. It was like a light bulb went on in his head.

"Yeah, why?" I replied.

"I met her a long time ago. My predecessor helped her make a," he paused, pointing at me. "Oh. That makes sense. I think my predecessor helped her bind your powers."

"That explains *a lot*. But that is not our biggest concern. Right now, we need to find out why this 'Frankenstein' is making the virus and why they needed the blood of the truest believer," Millie said.

"Could Frankenstein be a fucked-up nickname?" Nya asked.

"I certainly hope so." Millie sighed loudly, running her fingers through her hair.

A noise somewhere between a groan and a growl came out as I sat down on the curb. I tried to process exactly what had happened, the way the whole situation played out, and I couldn't. Regardless of what powers I had, I would never get used to death.

Especially death that happened right beside me.

What was happening that Lilly would rather die than face it?

"Why would she do that?" I asked no one in particular as I started to cry. "I mean, everyone does bad things. But if you try to do better and correct your mistakes, you can atone. Did she not see that if she helped us it could have helped her too?"

Millie sat down beside me. "Camille, Lilly did not get the nickname 'traitor' simply because she worked for the Kinkaid's. She did things, even to her own kind."

"*Especially* to her own kind," Nya chimed in.

"A good deed can't remedy *that*. She was involved in what may be the destruction of the human race as we know it." Millie continued, "I don't think she could live with her guilt."

"What exactly did she do? Other than this thing with the virus?"

"We can discuss it another time. What I will say is that Lilly Darling has enough blood on her hands that they may be permanently stained. That's not easy to come back from."

"Is that going to happen to me?"

Millie tried to smile and stroked my hair. "No. You acted in self defence."

"Bliss killed Lucia Kinkaid," I whispered to her.

"I figured. Did she have just cause?"

"Lucia had Bliss's brother beaten to death," I began. "That's why I have been so terrified. Because if they find out the truth...even if Tobias claimed her...."

I looked up at Nya and Eric, who were chatting amongst themselves and not paying attention. "You can't tell them. You can't tell anyone."

"I won't dear." She smiled and patted my back as I turned my gaze across the road. I saw something move in the shadows but couldn't focus on it.

A dark van pulled up on the curb across the street. It looked surprisingly similar to the one The Wild Boys had been driving that crazy night.

I hadn't spoken to October since I called her the night Bliss disappeared a week or so ago. I knew nothing about what she had found, or if she had gotten herself killed. That was a whole side of the story that I wanted to know more about, but with everything else going on, it would have to wait.

Two men in dark clothes got out of the van and headed into The Matador. I watched in amazement like some people watch the clean up after a car accident.

How are they going to get the body out?

One of the men came out a few minutes later carrying what looked like a duffel bag. It was hard to tell the shape.

"Where is the gurney?" I said quietly.

Millie put her hand on my shoulder. "They can't let anyone see a body come out of the club. It's a cloaking spell. I promise she is being treated respectfully."

"This is so messed up." I started to cry more as the truck pulled away. The world felt like it was crashing down around me, and I had no idea how to handle it. "She was our lead. What the fuck am I supposed to do now?"

Eric came over and held out his hand, pulling me to my feet. His warm hand in mine made me feel more grounded.

"You're a private investigator. This world may have magic, but standard rules still apply," he said.

"I don't understand."

"Tomorrow we investigate."

7.

True to his word, Eric was waiting for me in my office the next morning with coffee and donuts. It was nicer than flowers.

He was sitting in the chair with his computer on his lap. When I walked in, he looked up and smiled. "Morning sunshine."

I piled all my stuff in the corner, grabbed my laptop, and crawled over my desk to my chair.

"Morning. I did *not* sleep. Like at all. Peter Pan is scary when you really dissect the story," I replied, leaning across the desk and grabbing my coffee. It was strong but sweet and vanilla flavoured, just like I like it.

"I know it's hard to put it aside, but we can worry about what happened to Lilly later. Let's find your friend. What can you tell me about the last location she was at?"

"The address is in my phone. I tried to find someone to drive me that night, but I couldn't." I wasn't about to tell him that I went there by myself and threw rocks through the windows like a child.

"So let's go."

"Right now?"

"Yep. You got somewhere else to be?"

"Yeah. Here. *At work.*"

He smiled. "I already checked with Ramona. Our schedules are clear today."

"Why does that keep happening?"

"I don't understand."

"It seems like I've had zero appointments recently. What is up with that?"

"I don't think we have had any new clients this week. Chris and Ted are working on open cases. I already spoke to all three of them."

"You what now?"

"I told Chris and Ted I was looking into something about Mrs Tanner and needed your help. I didn't have to be so detailed with Ramona, who smiled and winked. We are free to go."

I took a big swig of my coffee. "We will need more caffeine. I am not sure I can get through the day without it."

"That's easy enough. Let's go."

We drove to suburbia, picking up more coffee on the way. I sipped it happily as we drove, smiling stupidly out the window as the scenery started to look familiar. I was so happy in my coffee fuelled state that it took me far longer than it should have to clue in to where we were.

"You been here before?" Eric asked as he slowed down and parked.

I looked at the houses on the street, and something clicked. I examined the smaller details and began to remember. In the daylight everything looked different than when I had come on my own.

"Yeah. I have," I answered. I blinked, and I was in the back seat of Ted's car with Fray. But not Fray—Noah. He was back to his high school self. He smiled at me, thanking Ted and I for dropping him off at his band practice.

"That…that…that is Eamon's house," I blurted out. "The fucking drummer of this fucking band that I went to high school with. *Our friends.* They are mine and Bliss's friends. Ted and I dropped him off here after Noah and I were studying at the library. I couldn't bring him to my house because Jesse would have lost his shit. They were practicing for the talent show where they got booed off the stage."

I took out my phone and got online, doing a quick title search on the house address. Sure enough, the house was owned by Eamon's parents.

Why didn't I do that when I went before?

I was here, in the dark mind you, but I didn't see it. My fear must have blinded me. Or maybe I didn't want to see it.

"Why were the Kinkaid's holding Bliss at her friend's

house?" he asked.

"Good question. Maybe we should go ask them."

I took a deep breath to calm myself, but I ended up hyperventilating instead. I bent over and tried to put my head between my knees, which was difficult while wearing a seat belt.

"What do I do?" Eric asked. "What do you want to do?"

"How could I be so stupid?" I blurted out. "He sings my favourite song at every fucking concert. He has a goddamn bishop tattoo, the chess piece, and has supposedly been in love with me since high school. He wanted me to be his girlfriend. He helped Bliss get into college. He was, or I thought he was, our friend. How could I not see he was playing us both?"

"You're not a psychic or clairvoyant. This is not your fault."

"But I should have fucking known. That's my job. As soon as I tracked the address and Google Earth searched the damn house, I should have known!Why do I keep getting played by these assholes?"

"This may be the wrong time to say this, but I must repeat it: *Boys.* You are dealing with *boys.*"

I sat up and stared at him. "You asked me why they would hold her at her friend's house. Let's go ask him."

"Are you sure that's a good idea?"

"It's a great idea. I am fucking done with getting kicked around. With getting played by sick excuses for people. He needs to be held accountable for his actions."

"I won't let you kill anyone."

"What the hell? I'm not going to kill him. That would be *too* easy. I am just going to make him pee his pants. Now, please take me to him or I will go on my own."

"What's the address?"

I banged on Fray's door as hard as I could. I was tired and annoyed, and I wanted answers.

Like, now.

"Cas. Hi!" Fray smiled brightly when he saw my face. That ball of energy I'd had to dig for was now at the forefront, easily coiling itself inside of my body like a tentacle. It reached out for him, knocking him in his chest hard enough to throw him back into his apartment, skidding towards the living room.

"What the hell!" Fray yelled. "Camille, what the—"

I wrapped that energy tentacle around his throat, pulling him up off the floor and dangling him in the air. I hadn't even thought about putting on my gloves.

"Did you think I wouldn't figure it out?" I snapped at him. "You held her at Eamon's parents' house, you dumbass. Did you think I wouldn't remember that Ted dropped you there? Am I that fucking transparent?"

Fray sniffled and choked, not saying a word. Eric stood beside me completely silent.

"*Where the fuck is Bliss, Noah!*" I screamed at him. My face felt hot from anger.

"I don't know! I'm sorry!" he sputtered, then started crying, the pathetic blubber of someone caught in their lie and scared shitless. "I didn't know this would happen!"

"Is this a joke to you? You're supposed to be her friend. She trusted you."

The crying got worse. I squeezed a little harder out of frustration. His eyes bugged out, and his face turned red. That little bit of emotion I had for him was gone. When I looked at him now, I felt sick to my stomach.

"Put him down so he can talk," Eric said flatly. He was right, even if I didn't want to hear it.

I slammed Fray into the ground, my energy retracting back into my body. He gasped for air and clutched at his throat.

"You should thank him," I told Noah, motioning at Eric. "If he hadn't spoken up, I would have popped your little head like a pimple and felt no ways about it."

Noah began to hyperventilate, crying hysterically. That once painfully handsome face was contorted in fear and anger in such a way it made him so completely repulsive that I turned away from him. I felt nothing for him as he blubbered on.

Not a damn thing.

He stumbled as he tried to get up, coming towards me. Eric put his hand on my shoulder, in an attempt to calm me, as I wrapped Noah in energy, holding him in place. This energy was different, it was something that turned much more solid that held him in place like he was trapped in ice or wet cement. He was completely frozen except his face.

"Either you tell me now or I will squeeze the answer out of you," I said to him calmly.

"Eamon got sick! We were so close. We would have lost our deal; lost *everything* we worked our whole fucking lives for if we hadn't helped them," Noah sputtered out. "All she said was that if we brought her some blood, she would cure Eamon. It was just a little blood! And she cured him. I didn't know what she was going to do! I didn't know they were going to take Bliss!"

"Who is *she*?"

"Nikki."

"You mean the fucking broad that answered your phone the other day? The girl that my stupid ass felt like shit about is the root of this nonsense? Great. I want her full name and phone number."

"I.... I...."

I walked over to his frozen figure and pulled his cell phone out of his pocket. "You still have not answered my first question. *Where the fuck is Bliss, Noah?!*"

"I don't know! They wouldn't tell me after she left Eamon's house. They said they wouldn't kill her!"

I laughed. "What they are planning to do is much, *much* worse."

I saved the contents of Noah's phone to his micro SD card and took it. Then I walked over to his laptop, which was sitting open on his coffee table, and copied its contents onto a flash drive I had on my keychain. I took pics of his IP address and any other numbers I could find that Q might use to get remote access if necessary.

He stared at me, panicked and immobile. His face wasn't as red, but it was blotchy from all his crying. His once perfect blue eyes were bloodshot and glazed over, bulging out of his head. He reminded me of a fish out of water left on the shore to die, flopping around gasping for air.

I stalked back to him as I scrolled through his contacts. "So which Nikki is she? There are a few in here. You should have some kind of code to keep your girls organized."

"Her name is Nikki Frank."

I walked over to him, getting as close as I could without being tempted to choke the life out of him.

"You and I are done. If anything happens to Bliss, I will kill you with my bare hands." I looked into his eyes as I calmly spoke. "If you continue to be honest with me, you might make it out of this. If Bliss is hurt in any way, you and your piece of shit friends better fucking leave town because *I will hunt you down and destroy you.* You are a horrible excuse for a person, and I am ashamed to know you."

I released him and held my ground. I waited to see if he would try anything. I was disgusted to even use my powers on him. "Did you bother to ask what the blood was for? Do you have any idea what you have done?"

C'mon asshole. Give me a reason.

I stood over top of him, and he occasionally turned his gaze to me as he crawled away.

Maybe now he would understand. Maybe now they

would understand not to mess with me.

"What the hell are you?" Noah blurted out when I finally turned and headed for the door.

"Not what," I called behind me as we walked out of the loft. "Who."

I sat down in the passenger seat of Eric's car and bent over, putting my head back between my knees. It was easier without a seat belt. I tried to breathe normally, but it was hard between horrified sobs.

How many people would die because those idiots wanted to keep their record deal? I should do the world a favour and kill him now before he did any other seriously dumb shit.

Praise Jebus! I never had sex with that clown! Hurray!

There was too much shit involved in this storm for me to process it all. I was angry and horrified all at the same time. What lengths was I willing to go to? What would I do to find Bliss?

Sure, I had thought about killing Fray back there, but would I? It may have made me feel better in the moment, but what good would it have done?

You would never bring about the end of the human race to save your friend. This is different.

I felt a warm hand on my back, and that warmth began to slowly spread through my body like syrup covering pancakes. I was calmer, and my thoughts became clearer.

"That's a nifty little trick," I said to Eric as I turned my head to face him. "Just so you know, *that* was the boy trouble."

His eyebrows raised. "Oh yeah? That's a bit of a surprise."

"Why? He's gorgeous. And a Rockstar. *Was* gorgeous. Now he makes me sick. Wow, I'm stupid."

"Sure, he's pretty, but it seems like that's all he is. I figured you could see right through his whole shtick. You're smarter than that."

"It was also kind of a rebound thing. He was the first guy to take an interest in me after my relationship ended. My ex was the only person who took an interest in me *ever,* other than my family. How pathetic is that, right? I'm a mess."

"Right. Ted told me a little about that. Hope you don't mind."

I sighed. "No, I don't mind that you know I have shitty taste in dudes! That's cool."

"*Boys,*" he said, ignoring my sarcasm. "You *clearly* need to start spending some time with men."

I sat up slowly and wiped my tears with my sleeve. "I am starting to think there is something wrong with me. Maybe I should've given Harold LeFaye my powers and saved myself from this shit."

"You couldn't have given him your powers. It's just not physically possible. If you somehow lost your powers, they would lie dormant until the next *Blanchmains* is born. He was full of shit."

I looked him in the eyes and fought back tears. He took one of my hands and held it with both of his.

"What do I do now?" I asked, and then the waterworks continued. He pulled me to him and hugged me tight. I buried my face in his neck and breathed deeply a few times, trying to calm myself, but the tears would not stop. My body shook as I sobbed.

I clung to him like a life preserver. I was embarrassed to be crying like that, but I could not let him go. Something inside me screamed that if I did, he would be gone, and I would be all alone. The darkness that always seemed to sit dormant inside me was ready to consume me if I let it.

He pulled back a bit, using his sleeve to wipe my tears. Looking into his eyes, I felt safe and good, like all this chaos would settle itself because of his presence. Like he would fix everything.

You dumb-dumb. You don't need a man to save you. You need to save yourself.

I took a breath, and then I leaned over and kissed him softly on the lips. When he did not react, I pulled away and felt my face flush. Had I misread his signals?

Oh God. I should have known he would never be interested in a girl like me.

Wow, Cas. Way to hit a home run.

"Oh God. I'm sorry. That was stupid of me." I pulled out of his grip, flailing my hands before using them to cover my overly embarrassed face. "I'm such a douchebag!"

I heard the car start, feeling the jolt as we started moving. I was tempted to jump out, do a full tuck and roll manoeuvre, just to avoid more embarrassment. I leaned my head against the passenger side window, keeping my face partially covered and turned away from him.

Ten minutes later, I finally got the courage to ask where we were going. I looked around outside to see if I recognized where we were.

He pulled into the lot of the small restaurant in the middle of High Park, a large municipal park in the west end of Toronto.

He got out of the car, without saying a word, and walked away. I was so confused. Was I supposed to wait? Or follow him? Or find my own way home?

He headed towards the rose garden. I wasn't about to sit here and look like an idiot not knowing what was going on. So I gathered my stuff and made sure he had his keys. I got out of the car, locking the doors behind me. I took a deep breath, stood up straight, and tried to walk with confidence as I followed him. But I probably looked like a toddler lost in the mall.

"Dude, what the hell?" I yelled when I found him. He was standing off near the edge of a path, in view of the garden and the pond.

"Stop talking," he said as he pulled me into his embrace, kissing me full on the lips.

Time stopped. The world around us faded, and all I could see, or feel, was him. His lips were soft and tender, and his touch made me feel like every part of my body was finally awake. I felt like a complete person for the first time in my whole life, like he was my missing piece. Like everything was beginning now, and my whole life up until that point was just the prologue.

Lots of people skip the prologue.

"What just happened?" I asked when we finally separated. I opened my eyes and stared deeply into his.

"Our first kiss was *not* going to be outside your former lover—"

"*I did not sleep with him.*"

"Sorry! Your former *paramour's* house. After you attacked him, I might add."

"But you let me think—"

He kissed me again, running his hand through my hair and cupping my head gently. His mouth opened slightly, and our tongues touched, sending a wave of heat through my body. I put my hand on his chest. I wanted to touch his skin. *All of it.*

I pulled away slightly, so I could see his face. "I have only ever been with one person. For real. My whole life."

"So?" he asked. "What does that have to do with anything?"

"I might be really bad at this." He laughed as I continued, "I have no clue what I am doing in life in general, and when it comes to romance stuff, I am *so* lost."

"Hey, I get it. Ted told me a bit about what happened. Ramona did too. I think she digs the idea of us together, by the way. Then I vetted him."

"You vetted my dead boyfriend?"

"Would you rather explain it?"

I thought for a moment. "No, I'm cool. Continue."

"Okay. Well, I think I have a clear picture of it. Him.

Whatever. Point is, you don't have to explain until you're ready."

"Speaking of Ted and Ramona, we should probably get back," I said, then I kissed him again. I did not want to stop, but I knew my phone would start ringing soon. People would be looking for us eventually. We were supposed to be working after all.

"We will have to plan a day of just you and me. No one else's drama or anything else."

"Saturday."

He smiled. "Okay. Saturday."

"We should also keep this quiet for now."

"Agreed. Don't know if Ted and Chris would be kosher with it. And I don't want Millie and Nya to be suspicious of my motives."

I smiled. "What are your motives?"

"You. Just you." He kissed me again, but this time he pulled away first. Then he took my hand and started guiding me back to his car.

We held hands as we drove back to the office. I'd held Jesse's hand in a similar way. That felt like eons ago. It came as a great surprise to me that I was happier now than I had ever been, even though we had only had a moment.

"Maybe we should spend the rest of the day looking into Nikki Frank," he said as we pulled up outside L&B.

"Could 'Frank' be short for 'Frankenstein'?" I asked.

"I don't know. But we'll find out."

We parted ways at my office door. I wanted to kiss

him goodbye, but I just watched him as he walked down the hall and disappeared around the corner.

I went straight to work finding out who Nikki was and if she was this 'Frankenstein'. The flash drive clicked as I slid it into my laptop, and with the punch of a key, the contents of Fray's phone began downloading. As they transferred over, I opened my desk drawer to find a card reader for the micro SD I took from him.

I looked at my computer screen, and my eyeballs felt strange. I blinked, and it seemed like the edges of my vision shook. My peripheral vision started to become milky.

I closed my eyes tight, then opened them again, and it stopped. I would have to ask Eric about that later. What was happening to me?

A darkness appeared in the corner of my office, a strange shadow I had not seen before. I blinked hard, squeezing my eyes shut again, and it was gone.

I needed to get my eyes checked. Maybe I was getting glaucoma. Or having an aneurism.

Calm down nutjob.

I could not find anything about Nikki or Nicole Frank. The phone number Fray had for her was registered to LaBelle Waterford Industries. I texted Q and asked her if she could find me any dirt on Nicole 'Nikki' Frank and gave her the phone number.

A short time later there was a quick knock at my door, which was the signal from Ted that it was time to go.

I gathered up my things and quickly texted Eric that Ted and I were leaving. I knew I couldn't run to his office and kiss him goodbye. It hurt my heart a bit.

He was at the end of the hallway by Lewis's office when I stepped out with my gear. He smiled and waved. I did the same and tried not to look too eager.

"So how was your time out with Eric?" Ted asked when we got in the car.

"Great! I like him a lot," I said as he started driving. "I mean, he's cool. I like him."

Ted laughed. "Don't tell Lewis, but I like him too. I'm happy you two are getting along."

"Me too. It's been a welcome distraction."

"Have you heard from Bliss?"

I exhaled loudly. "No."

"What do you think is going on?"

"I think Tobias Kinkaid got his claws in her, and Fray helped him sink them in."

"How do Bliss and Fray have anything to do with the Kinkaid's?"

"Ren."

"And Fray?"

I groaned. "That is a long story. But he is *not* who I thought he was. I won't be socializing with him anymore."

He smiled weakly at me, and I nodded.

"No. No. It's okay. I'm good. It was a harsh realization at first, but I made peace with it. Better I figured it out now before I got too attached," I began. "People are weird and horrible."

"I wish I could say they get better, but they don't. Age only hardens people in their foolish ways."

He pulled up at the house, and we unloaded our gear and went inside in silence.

I hauled all my stuff up to my room, and as soon as I put my bag down at my desk, my phone started beeping.

I went to check it, and my eyes started vibrating again, thin milky edges building around my vision. I blinked hard.

I sat down on the bed and blinked again, wiping my eyes.

It felt like there was a weird fluid building around my eyes that I couldn't wipe off. Maybe I was getting cataracts. Strange shapes floated into my vision, and I wanted to vomit. Hard. The floating objects were giving me the spins.

I took a deep breath and tried to steady myself. I was tempted to lay on the floor.

I wished I could talk to Lilly Darling. I had so many questions. She could probably put some of the pieces together that I couldn't, like how this Nikki Frank was connected to the Kinkaid's. If she was involved in making the virus, it was safe to assume she was some kind of scientist.

"Bitch is a lot more than some kind of scientist," a female voice chimed in, making me jump.

I turned slowly towards my desk, where Lilly Darling sat cross legged. Her long dark hair hung down around her face like a sheet, and her eyes were wide and stared at me like she might burn a hole in my head.

"Fuck me gently with a chainsaw," I sputtered out. I blinked hard, hoping I was hallucinating. That haze in my eyes was gone; everything appeared to have gone back to normal.

She wrinkled her nose. "Violence. Nice. You'll need it to deal with Dr. Frankenstein."

"How did you get here?"

"You summoned me, dumbass. Or did the poor little prophecy girl forget she had powers?"

"I have never summoned anyone. I didn't even know I had powers until a few weeks ago when my mom's family unbound them. It's a long story," I took a deep breath. "I watched you die."

Her head cocked to one side. "So the natural order of your prophecy was disrupted? Uh oh."

"What do you mean 'uh oh'? And let me add, I am *freaking* out right now that I just randomly summoned you."

I covered my mouth and tried not to hyperventilate. She watched me like someone watches an animal in a cage. What I understood of the world, my world, just crumbled.

I watched her die.

"Wow. You have no idea, do you? I figured with your parents' murder—"

"My what now?" That made me focus for about a minute. "What do you know about my parents?" I asked.

She studied my face again. "That is a conversation for

another day. Once you deal with Dr. Frankenstein, we can talk about what I know about your parents."

"Why do you keep saying 'Dr. Frankenstein'? Are they like some kind of crazy mad scientists or something? Can we get back to the fact that *I watched you die*?"

She rolled her eyes. "Because *they are*, dummy. Nicole Frank *is* Nicole Frankenstein. Her grandpa is the legit Victor Frankenstein from the book, which was really the world's first true crime story, and no one believed it. It's just as fucked as it sounds. I met Victor."

"You have *got* to be *fucking kidding me!*" I yelled. "Do you expect me to believe this shit? Frankenstein? Really? This is insane." I gestured wildly at her. "I finally lost it."

"Alright, *white hands*. Descendant of the nine sisters of Avalon. Shove your head up your ass a little farther, sweetheart."

"Aren't you the girl who claims to be related to Peter Pan? You have *no* right to mock me. And you! *You* betrayed your own people! To work for the goddamn Kinkaid's! AND I watched you die! And you're here! How am I supposed to believe a word you say?"

Lilly threw her hands up in the air. "Fine! You want to be like that? Fine! Bring me back when you come to your senses. But ask Millie and the fucking Merlin what happens when someone fucks with a prophecy. *Ask them*. Then fucking call me back when you know I'm not lying, and we can talk more about Frankenstein."

It was like my vision snapped, the world had turned into elastic that had been pulled and snapped back into place. I blinked, and Lilly was gone.

That's it. I'm done.

My phone rang forty five minutes later. It took that noise to bring me back to reality. What had just happened, what Lilly Darling had just told me, was mind boggling. I wasn't sure how to function. I was in the fetal position on my bed, trying to think.

Then I heard Lilly's voice in my head.

The dead girl who had just spoke to me.

Ask Millie. And the fucking Merlin.

"Hello?" I picked up on the third ring.

"Hey, Camille. It's Millie." She sounded like she was walking outside. "Are you busy tonight? I got word on another game. And this is a big one."

"Can I ask you something?"

"Absolutely. What's up?"

"Do you know anything about what happens if you disrupt the natural order of a prophecy?"

Silence. "Where is this coming from?"

"Something Lilly Darling said today."

"Lilly?"

"I'm not sure how I did it, but I summoned Lilly Darling."

"Holy shit, Camille! That's huge!"

"I know. She told me to ask you about this prophecy thing. She said some other shit that I don't quite believe...she even said something about my parent's murder. I swear on everything that is holy I have lost my fucking marbles. I watched her die, and yet she was sitting on my desk."

"She did? Well, Lilly is a lot of things, but a liar is not one of them. Let me look into this prophecy thing. I think I know what she means, but I want to double check. Ask Eric too. I will come and pick you up tonight, if you're free. I hope you're free."

"I am. What time are you coming?"

"I'll be there in an hour. Make sure you bring your gloves. It's mandatory."

Ted was asleep in his chair when I came downstairs. Empty beer bottles were strewn on the floor beside his feet. The house seemed empty, and while normally I would be happy that Ted had some time to himself, something inside me did not want to leave him alone tonight. But I had to figure this out. Millie said this was important. I had to regain my composure to find Bliss.

I wrote Ted a note and told him I was doing more cooking with Millie, and I would call him later. I signed it with I love you. It was important to tell him that. I was sure that I never said enough.

While I waited on the porch for Millie, I texted Eric and told him about Lilly and about the poker game. He said he would meet us there and not to worry. I had to refrain from flipping out. I hated it when people said don't worry. A series of anger-fuelled rants ran through my mind as I stared at my phone, deciding if I should reply to his text or not.

My life is chaos, and you're telling me not to worry? I see dead people, and you say don't worry?

A light sprinkle of snow began to fall from the sky, distracting me from my thoughts. Canada had very defined seasons, and I should have known when there was a slight chill at night that winter was coming. I quietly went back inside and grabbed a jacket in case the weather got worse.

Millie arrived, and I carefully walked out to her SUV; there wasn't enough snow yet that it needed shovelling, but it was slippery.

"Hi!" Nya was oddly chipper when I climbed in the back. Millie pulled away and drove off as soon as I closed the door.

"Hey," I said, putting on my gloves. My hands were already turning white.

"You good, dude?" Nya asked, watching me through the visor mirror as she applied her pink lipstick.

"No, but that's not news. Where are we going?"

Millie smiled. "More poker. Only this game is often frequented by vampires. They'll know *something* I am sure."

"I'm in the mood to break stuff if they want to make life difficult."

"Did Eric have any insight about what Lilly said?"

Nya's eyebrows raised. "When did Lilly say...?" She turned and looked at me. "Did you summon Lilly?"

"You never told her?" I asked Millie.

"Not my news," Millie replied.

"Yeah, I don't know how I did it, but I summoned Lilly.

She said a bunch of shit. But the important part was that disrupting my prophecy is a big deal. Oh, and supposedly the Kinkaid's have the real Frankenstein working for them."

"Huh." Nya's gaze went back to the mirror and her makeup. .

"That's all you got is 'huh'?"

"Did you ask Eric?"

"Yep. He said don't worry."

"Urgh. I hate that."

"I know, right? Do you know what she was talking about?"

Nya looked at Millie, then back at me. "I think I might but…"

"But what? Spit that shit out already!"

"There is this thing, but we don't know if it's true or not. Prophecy's don't just *happen* all the time so we have no proof."

"Nya, I'm not in the goddamn mood. Lilly was already cagey enough. Just tell me!"

"Alright! Fuck! There is this story that if a prophecy is not allowed to run its natural course a—"

"Marie would have known that. She wouldn't take that risk," Millie interrupted.

"*Just spit it out*!" I yelled.

"A demon is formed!" Nya blurted out. "Jesus. There is no proof that it's true. It's just a story."

"Harold would know that too. Why would either of them risk it?" Millie continued. "It makes no sense."

"Well, once we're done with this bullshit, I will summon my mom and ask her," I snapped, my frustration and anger turning into a hard ball inside my chest. "Since when do demons exist? I have too many questions that I cannot handle the answers to right now, especially walking into what we are about to walk into. My head is going to explode. And we haven't even addressed the Frankenstein mess. But if *demons* exist, why the fuck not, right?"

Nya smiled. "Let's tackle one bag of bullshit at a time, Cas. Now, just a quick warning."

"Son of a bitch!" I cursed loudly and slid down in my seat."For fuck's sake! What now?!"

"Vampires are temperamental. Just so you're aware. They think they're superior and can be a bunch of bitchy little girls."

"I met the Kinkaid kids. I get it."

"We keep warning you to prepare for shit to go south. This would be the place for that to happen. What happened at Burnt Offerings is nothing compared to what could happen here. Is Eric meeting us there?" I nodded as she continued. "Good. We will need all the help we can get."

"Great. Just great. When did my life turn into this insane cluster fuck? I need to find Bliss. I can't. I just can't."

Millie gave me a compassionate smile. "We'll figure it out. Just breathe."

"And put your big girl pants on," Nya added. "Because we're here."

We went in a back door in an alley that was propped open with a brick. I wasn't sure exactly where we were; everything was covered in a thin layer of white snow that made it seem clean and pure. When I looked around more closely, I figured out we were in Greek Town, part of the east side of Toronto and far enough that I was out of my element. The last time I had been in this neighbourhood was a disastrous process serving incident with Ted.

As soon as we stepped in the door, the hair on the back of my neck stood up and my hands began to throb. I put them in my pockets and tried my best to relax and breathe. I had to keep my cool.

Eric crept up behind us just as we stepped into the hallway beyond the door. He put his hand on my shoulder, and I immediately calmed down.

"My hands hurt," I said quietly to him, showing him that I had my gloves on.

"Hello to you too," he said. "Since when?"

"Since we stepped in the door. There is something fishy going on."

I held onto Eric's arm as we walked down the hallway into a smoke-filled room. A woman walked passed us with long dark hair. She was wearing a backless shirt that showed off an enormous tattoo, and an extremely short skirt and heels. I couldn't help but stare at her.

"Holy shit, it's you!" I heard a male voice exclaim. I got goose bumps. "Hey, new girl! I knew I sensed something about you."

I turned my head and smiled at Tobias Kinkaid, trying

to keep my expression neutral. The woman with the long dark hair finally turned her head, and I saw her face.

"Bliss?" my voice was small and quiet like a surprised child. We made eye contact; her pupils were so dilated that her irises looked black. She could barely keep her eyes open they were so red. I was sure the colour drained from my face, and it was just as white as my hands.

She stared blankly at me like she had no clue who I was, then turned and walked back over to Tobias. She perched on a stool beside him, her face eye level with the table. Her already long hair looked as if it had grown a foot more since the last time I saw her as it now reached her waist. Tobias touched the top of her head affectionately, like one would pet a dog or a cat.

She should just sit on the floor and get it over with. Where was her collar and leash?

I stood there for a few minutes, completely dumbfounded as Eric and Nya pulled me to the other side of the room.

"So that's her, huh?" Nya said quietly to me.

"That *was* her," I replied. I had to fight to keep my voice level. "I don't know what the hell he has her on, but that's *not* the same person. And what's with the massive tat on her back? Is that part of it?"

I watched as my friend sat beside that piece of shit, on her little stool like a prized fucking puppy, and made goo-goo eyes at him. She kept reaching out for him, and he would shoo her like a fly buzzing around his head.

"I have to go talk to her," I said as I broke free of the

others and walked over to my friend.

"Hey!" I tried to seem as cheerful as I could. "I haven't heard from you in a few days, how are you?"

Bliss glanced at me, half smiling. "Oh, I'm good."

"Can we talk for a sec?"

Bliss looked at Tobias. He glanced at me briefly, and then nodded like he was giving her permission. Should have patted her on the head and gave her a treat while he was at it.

She got up and we stepped away, not out of earshot, but far enough that I could say what I needed to without Tobias getting involved.

"Are you okay? I haven't heard from you in a while. Some shit went down with Fray and we *really* need to talk about it."

"I am fine, Camille. I don't have time to hear about your stupid boy problems, nor do I want to," Bliss snapped. Her face contorted into this angry snarling expression that made me take a step back. The expression on her face, in her eyes, made it seem like she was disgusted to even look at me. Like my presence annoyed her.

"Okay, well, do you want to come with me to—"

"I don't want to go anywhere with *you*. You're a pathetic loser. I am exactly where I need to be." Her words stung, just as she had intended.

"What? I don't...I don't understand."

She sighed loudly and rolled her eyes. "God, you are as stupid as Jesse always said. Do I need to spell it out for you? *We're not friends, Camille.* Now get out of my face."

She turned and went back to Tobias, leaving me standing there like the asshole I was.

I quickly turned and walked back over to Eric and Nya before anyone could see my face. Millie was off by the bar talking to Liam Fitzpatrick.

I stood beside them and took a calming breath. I would not cry. I could not cry. I already looked stupid enough, if I started crying now that would make me exactly what she said I was. A pathetic fucking loser.

"What just happened?" Eric asked quietly. I looked him in the eyes, and Bliss's words rang in my ears. I felt darkness swirl around me.

He could never love someone like me.

He reached out for me, and I pulled away. I lowered my gaze to the floor and bit back my tears. Using every bit of energy I had, I tried to imagine a hole in the floor beneath my feet that would swallow me up.

Tobias Kinkaid began to laugh. And that darkness took on a shape.

The sound was so painful it felt like I had been stabbed a thousand times in the back. My worst nightmares were now becoming fully formed.

I had no friends. Because I am a pathetic loser who doesn't deserve any.

I am nothing without Jesse.

When the rumble started, it was almost inaudible. Then things in the room began to shake. I could hear the furniture as it pitter patted on the floor like dozens of tiny dancing feet, and the rattle of the paintings as they tapped on the walls.

The darkness smiled.

"Who the hell is doing this?" someone yelled. My eyes remained down.

"*She* probably is," I heard Bliss's disgusted voice snap. I assumed she pointed at me. I felt people come towards me, and the shaking got louder. Eric clamped his hand around my wrist. His power crept up my arm, but my energy wasn't interested and pushed it away.

"Hey!" An angry voice got closer to me. "Cut that shit out!" Eric's grip tensed.

I lifted my head, looking the man, who was easily three times my size and thundering towards me like an angry hippo, in the eye. I smiled sweetly, then used every bit of power I had to fling him across the room. It also flung all the furniture and several other people. Including Tobias and Bliss.

I hope I killed him.

I hope I killed them both.

Eric yanked hard on my arm. "You need to chill."

"No," I said calmly.

Another large man started coming at us. I turned my gaze to him, that coil of energy that had grabbed Fray shot out like a bullet and tried to shove the man towards the ceiling. But he put up a fight, using whatever magic he had to keep his feet on the ground. I felt his power begin to stir inside him like the beginnings of a thunderstorm, and I pushed at him again to try to keep him from doing anything.

"What did she say to you?" Eric asked.

"The truth. That I am a pathetic loser and have no friends. That she and I were never friends."

"Cas...."

"*Save it.* Either help me or leave."

"It's in your best interest to leave. Now. Even if the three of us help you, we can't take this on. We need to run. Now."

"Take them and go."

"I am not leaving you here."

"Why do you care? It's not like you could give a shit about a pathetic loser like me. All you care about is my prophecy shit," I growled at him. So many emotions were swirling through me that they were competing for which should take priority, which was causing the energy that fuelled my powers to go into high gear.

"Is that what you really think?"

"I think a lot worse than that, but that is the easiest to vocalise."

He took a deep breath then turned away from me. Which is exactly what I thought he would do. Expecting him to do something different only set me up for disappointment. The furniture continued to shake, and people began to get up and leave.

"Camille, what the hell are you doing?" Millie's frightened voice snapped me back into reality. She stepped in front of Eric so all I could see was her. "Camille, I get that you are upset. But you can't do this. I know you thought she was your friend, but *it's not worth your life.*"

Millie put her hands on my shoulders and looked in my eyes. "If you do this now, you can't come back from it. The whole world will know."

I got a flash of my mother's face, and thought about what she had done to protect me from all of this. I liked to think she and I would have been friends. That now that I was an adult we could have hung out like people. Maybe even been girlfriends.

She would have only hung out with me because she had to. That's what moms do.

I heard the sirens. Eric and Nya disappeared. The rest of the world went on. But Millie and I stood there. She stayed with me, and so did the darkness.

Even when the cops came, Millie stayed. She smiled at me like a mother would as they cuffed us both. She continued to smile at me when they put us in separate squad cars and drove her away.

8.

TODAY
BACK TO WHERE WE STARTED...

"My hands? It's weird, right?" I said to Kiera, showing her my white hands. "It's a circulation thing, I think. It's called Raynaud's syndrome. I have to go back to the doctor."

I had checked it out ahead of time, in case I ever needed to explain my hands to anyone not magical. I needed a plausible reason. This was the best I could find.

"You do. Because that's weird," Kiera replied. "Are you sure you're ok? Because that's pretty close to the colour of dead bodies. You really need to talk to your doctor."

"Yeah, the blood just randomly stops running to your digits. Apparently, it can also happen in your nose and ears. White means it's not severe. When it turns blue that means it's bad," I explained. "If you uncuff me and give me my bag, I can give you Jesse's phone. And can

I have my gloves? This shit happens because my hands are cold. I need to warm them up."

She pointed at my hands again. "Are you trying to slip your cuffs?"

"What? No! Why would I...?" I looked down at my hands, the cuffs now hung loosely like a set of bangles. Oops."I guess the arresting officer didn't do them up that tight. You should talk to those uniform officers, Kiera. If I was a regular perp I could have slipped my cuffs and attacked you."

"Alright there, Bonnie without Clyde," she quipped. "Why are you not more bothered by this? Your lack of emotion for being arrested scares me."

"It shouldn't. I'm not emotional because I have done nothing wrong. My only crime is being in the wrong place at the wrong time. I can explain it all. I have nothing to hide. Millie was only there because of me. She did nothing wrong either." I bit my tongue and tried my best not to ramble, which would have been a dead giveaway that I was lying.

Kiera groaned and shook her head. I put my hands on the table and rubbed them together in an attempt to warm them. She wrote something else in the file, and then leaned over the table and uncuffed me.

"Don't take this as a kindness. I am letting you go because there is nothing to hold you, or Philomina LeFaye. I know you well enough to know that if there was something to bust you for, it would take work to find it. I want to trust you. But I am watching you. If I see or hear anything that I don't like, you're done. Got it? I will book your ass and feel no ways about it. I should have let you spend the night in a holding cell. You don't get special favours because you're a Bishop."

I smiled sweetly. "Not even 'cuz I'm your favourite?"

"Don't push your luck. Let me get your stuff, and I will take you home."

"What about Millie?"

"I informed her that I would escort you home. She wants you to phone her later."

I smiled. "Okay. As long as she is safe."

"She will be heading home shortly. Now, wait here. I will be right back." She took the file and left the room.

Would I actually have snooped in the file if I'd had the chance? If I would have gotten caught, my free pass would've been revoked with lightening speed!

We sat in silence on the way home. I didn't have much to say anyhow. I had given Jesse's phone to Kiera before we left the station, and I didn't want to nervous talk. Which was something I did often, and if I wanted her to believe me I had to keep my mouth shut.

She hugged me goodbye when we pulled up out-front of the house.

"I expect more from you, Cas. I know you're going through a lot," she began, "But don't let it fuck up your life. It's not what he would have wanted."

I laughed. "Do you mean Jesse? He would have wanted to *live*, Kiera. Turns out he didn't give much of a shit about me. Only what I could do for him."

She made this expression at me that was best described as an awe-poor-you face.

"Don't do that. I do not need pity. I'm a big girl." I kissed her on the cheek and opened the car door. "Let me know when you guys have a suspect. Anything you need, just let me know."

"You got any ideas on that, Cas?" she asked.

I faltered. "Not at the moment. Why?"

"You did so well with Morris Ludlow I figured you had already opened a file."

"Nah. I am not convinced he was murdered. So, no reason to look."

She shrugged. "I see your point. Maybe another day I will show you a reason."

"Don't you have people for that? Like cops and shit?"

"Maybe they're not as good as you. Have you ever thought about going to the police academy? You could be my apprentice."

Something popped up in my mind, and I hesitated as to whether to mention it to Kiera. If Bliss and I weren't friends anymore, I didn't need to protect her secret. After tonight, I should put it on a billboard.

"Hey, Kiera. Can you do something for me?"

She smiled. "Is it legal?"

"Absolutely. I want you to find out if Melissa 'Bliss' Fiori is an undercover cop or not. Keep it between us."

"Why would you ask me that?"

"Because she told me she was, and I want to know if that was a lie, like half the other shit that she told me."

I hugged her again and got out of the car.

"Is that a good idea? I mean, if you're really done with her and her situation, do you really want to know?"

"I think it would help me get passed it. All I want is a yes or no. You don't have to tell me if she's an undercover either. Just 'is she a cop'? Yes or no. Easy peasy."

She smiled at me. "I'll look into it. Especially if you'll seriously consider going to the police academy."

I rolled my eyes. "Thanks for the ride."

"I wish it was under better circumstances."

I shovelled the front walk and the driveway before I went in the house. It gave me the opportunity to calm down and clear my head.

It was earlier than I thought. Ted was asleep in his chair, and he stirred when I kissed him on the forehead. I whispered to him that I was taking a beer, grabbed a bottle out of the fridge, and went to my room.

I got my phone out of my purse and sat down on my bed. Opening the bottle, I took a swig. I wasn't a fan of beer, but today I would make an exception. It would raise a few eyebrows if I went in the liquor cabinet. One beer I could pass of as a passing urge, hard liquor not so much.

Too bad we didn't have any wine. I could add that to my to do list for tomorrow.

My eyes started to feel weird again, and this time I knew what it meant. So I breathed deeply and let it happen.

"Is now a good time to say I told you so?" Lilly asked.

"Why the fuck didn't you tell me about Bliss?" I asked. "Warn me? Anything?"

"Would you have listened?" she said, and I started crying. "Look, she's a lost cause. She's tangled in a web that you *do not* want to get snagged in. Trust me. Focus on other friends."

I started crying harder. "Don't you get it? I don't have any other friends! I'm pathetic."

"Pathetic according to who? Did that vamp tramp call you pathetic? You realize you're bothered by an insult from a walking vampire toy, right? That is *far* more pathetic than whatever lame insult she called you."

I tried to inhale calmly. "You have no idea."

"Who are those people you were rolling with?"

"Millie and Nya are le Fay. They're my mom's people. And Eric...well, every guy I have ever liked has had a hidden agenda. I'm sure he does too."

"Did you like that clown from that band? The pretty one?"

"I went to high school with him. He was my lab partner. He sung that stupid song for me. It was silly. Like a teenage crush. What the fuck do you know about Fray anyway? How did you know I know him?"

"Your expression at the Matador said it all. Either you knew him personally or you fangirled. Hard. And I know it's his and his band's stupid fault there's a fucking virus. That's enough. That shithead is a waste of space. You can do so much better. I don't even know you, and I know you can do better. I should have poisoned them all or something. Just wiped their useless asses from the earth before they could do more damage."

"He told me he did it to save his friend."

She laughed. "And that makes it okay? He can turn us all into cattle, but as long as *his friend* is okay it's acceptable? Fuck him."

"Cattle?"

"That's the point of the virus. They're turning us into superfood. Like the flesh equivalent of kale."

"I thought they were making vampires."

"No. They are too keen on their elitist bullshit. Only the crème de la crème get chosen to be one of *them*. Like they're fucking Kardashians or some shit."

I took another sip of my beer. "I can't deal with this shit. Can we just put a lid on all this? Like push pause or some shit?"

"Sorry, dude. Welcome to the trip. It gets heavy. But you should be used to all this by now—"

"I have only known for a few weeks! My mom bound my goddamn powers, told me nothing about any of this, and then she died."

She chuckled. "I know, I know. She told me all about it."

"Excuse me? What do you mean she told you? And why is it funny?"

"Oh. Shit. I didn't even think about that. You haven't spoken to her yet, have you?"

"No. Of course not," I said.

I was about to say more, when it felt like someone ran an ice cube up my spine. I jumped, and that flash of cold took over my body. I felt the dark presence. That same darkness I had felt at the club. It tried to wrap itself around me like a blanket.

"Did you just feel that?" I asked, spinning around and looking for whatever it was. As quickly as it had appeared, it was gone.

"No, dude. I can't feel shit! Did you hit your head or something? You're a light weight if you're already buzzing." She watched me as I sat back down on my bed. "I guess I can *Karate Kid* your ass. You look like you could use the help."

"*Karate Kid*? What the fuck are you talking about?"

"I can teach you, dumbass! There is shit that Millie and the Merlin are too fucking vanilla to show you." She laughed to herself. "Millie and the Merlin. Sounds like a shitty band."

I shrugged and took another sip of my beer. "Sure. Why not? My life is already pretty weird. Why not have a ghost teach me magic? Sounds great! I got some questions about my mom though. You will need to explain about her murder."

"Save them. Soon enough you can ask her yourself."

My phone beeped with a text from a number I did not know.

All the message said was 'I'm sorry. This was the only way I could save us all.'

9.

When I woke up the next morning, I thought I would feel different.

My already screwy world had once again been flipped on its head. Bliss and Noah Fray had come back into my life and almost as quickly were gone. I was pleased that I had found out the truth about Fray before I had done something I would regret. I already felt like a fool, it would have been much worse if I had slept with him.

The Bliss thing was painful. It made me sad. I couldn't begin to understand how someone would want to be possessed the way Tobias was possessing her. She wasn't a person anymore. She was an object. Getting played always hurt. I needed to figure out what was wrong with me that it keeps happening. Because it wasn't just about not inviting these people into my life, but figuring out what makes me so attractive to them.

I wondered if either Bliss or Fray had sent that text.

And, really, did I care? It was just a ploy to suck me in. I was not falling for it.

Nope. Not falling for it. Jesse used to do the same shit.

That was *always* how I got played. Some stupid text would tug at my foolish heartstrings, and I would allow him to speak to me and get sucked back in. Jesse could play me like a musical instrument. I was not doing that again.

Regardless of how painful it was, I didn't feel different. I couldn't help but wonder if I was numb. If I had finally reached my bullshit limit. Something had to give, and maybe I had finally cracked.

I got a text from Kiera while I was eating breakfast.

"Anything important?" Ted asked. He was sitting beside me at the kitchen table. Cuddy was on my other side. They were both happily eating the eggs and bacon Ted had made, I assumed to cure his hangover.

"No. Just Kiera. I had asked her to look into something for me," I replied.

"Anything I need to know about?"

"No. Nothing major."

"Did you finally get a hold of Bliss?"

"Yeah, I found her. She's not who I thought she was."

"Oh? What happened?"

I sighed. "She's hooked up with Tobias Kinkaid. And she is clearly on..." I glanced over at Cuddy, "something."

"I'm 18 years old, Cas. And I have seen Breaking Bad. You don't need to do that," Cuddy said with an eye roll.

"So maybe Jesse was right about her after all?"

I put down my fork and turned and looked at him. "Well, that's a first!"

"Hey, he gets one," he said. "I am quite shocked that a Fiori would hook up with a Kinkaid."

"Well, I am absolutely fucking disgusted. But, hey, what the fuck do I know?" Both men looked shocked as I spoke.

"Reign in those f-bombs when we get to the office, please. I get that you are upset, but cussing is not appropriate," Ted said.

"I'm good. It's out of my system. I just feel like an asshole that I *believed* her and Fray were my friends." Unless that text was true. But I'm not getting sucked in.

Ted gently pat my shoulder. "You were in a bubble for a long time. This is all stuff you should have gone through ages ago but didn't because you were so focused on Jesse. It'll be okay, I promise. And hey, maybe you'll make friends with Eric eventually. He's a good guy."

I would very much like to be his friend, and more.

But I may have fucked that up before it even started.

We left shortly after that, dropping Cuddy at school on the way to the office. Rollo's car was in the school lot. I hadn't read the text from Kiera yet, so I scanned it quickly when we pulled into the L&B parking lot.

It was as I had suspected. There was no record of a Bliss or Melissa Fiori anywhere, other than a sealed juvenile record. Kiera reassured me that she knows the officer who runs the entire undercover department, and he told her that there was no Fiori anywhere. She even found a picture of Bliss on Facebook that she showed him, and he said no. Then she ran it through their employee database, and nothing. Bliss was not, and never had been, a cop.

Of course she isn't, you gullible moron.

I texted Lemme and asked her if she ever got that secondary data from my other contact, and she replied, 'Not yet. Is it coming soon?' and I swore at my phone. Either that text was bullshit or not her.

"Everything okay?" Ted asked as we got out of the car.

"What? Yeah. Sorry. Kiera had a question about Jesse's phone," I said as we got out. "She picked it up from me last night when I was out. I was going to give her his spare charger, and I forgot."

"Well, she knows where you live if she really needs it," he replied. He held the door open for me, and we both headed inside.

The waiting room was empty, and I could hear Ramona humming to herself as she made coffee in the break room. Ted smiled and waved as he headed to his office. I thought about going and talking to Ramona. Her motherly disposition and kind words always made me feel better when I was upset. But I decided against it and headed for my office instead.

I stopped, took a deep breath, and opened my door. The room smelled like fresh coffee, and Eric sat in one of my chairs with his feet up on my desk, messing with his phone.

"Good morning," I said nervously, closing the door behind me. I slid over my desk to my chair, trying very hard not to knock over the two coffee's he had brought.

"Good morning. How was the big house?" he asked, not looking up from his phone.

I shrugged. "Fine. I didn't get charged. Clearly, since my head is not outside on a pike. Millie is fine too."

"I know. She phoned me. Why didn't you?"

"I figured after what happened last night you wouldn't want to talk to me."

"Should I talk to you?"

"I don't know if I would. But, as you can see by the supposed *friend* I have been chasing around, I am not the best judge of character."

"She is not worth it. You should focus on other friends."

I laughed. "Funny, that is exactly what Lilly said. The sad part is, I don't have any other friends. It was her and that dude. The fuckboy with the loft. That's why I got so upset. Because what she said hit the nail on the head."

He finally looked up at me. "You have me."

My eyes began to glaze over with tears. "I do?"

"Do you really think I am going to abandon you because you flipped out? I am not pleased that we could have gotten hurt, and you and Millie got arrested, but I'm not going anywhere, Cas."

I climbed back out from behind my desk and curled up on his lap, leaning my head on his shoulder. I took a deep breath, taking in his smell. The joy that I felt that he didn't storm out of my office was huge, but I tried to keep my face neutral. I didn't want to look like a lovesick teenager. The warmth of his body was comforting, it made me feel safe.

"Thank you," I told him. It took every ounce of strength I had to not cry.

"You're welcome." He wrapped his arms around me and hugged me. It was better in that moment than any kiss. "Well, now that we found her what do we do?"

"She lied to me."

"I know. She's—"

"No. She told me she's an undercover cop, so I would tell her what I had found out about the virus. She's not."

"Are you sure?"

"Absolutely. My cousin looked into it. And she was thorough."

"Huh. So I guess we know what we're doing now."

"What?"

"We're vetting Bliss Fiori."

When I kissed him on the cheek he turned his head, and we had a proper kiss. That warm wonderful feeling I'd had the first time we kissed was back, and I wished we weren't at work.

"Is that one of your powers?" I asked as we separated.

"What?"

"That your touch calms people down and makes them feel good."

"No, not at all. But I am happy to hear that. I take it as a compliment." He hugged me close to his body. "So, is

Fiori Spanish?"

"As far as I know."

"Maybe she's a *bruja*. You'd think that was something Lilly Darling would have picked up on. She never mentioned it?"

"That's a good point. Lilly said nothing about Bliss. Hiding something magical from me is one thing, but she also hid it from Lilly and the Kinkaid's. Which reminds me, the last time I summoned Lilly, I felt something weird."

He chuckled. "Yeah. She's a ghost."

"No. It was something else." I kissed his cheek again, then climbed back over my desk to my chair. "It was a cold chill up my spine, then like a blanket of darkness surrounded me. It felt like a physical presence, but it was entirely made of the darkest parts, not just of me, but of everything."

His expression was blank as he thought about what I said. "I don't know what to tell you. There is the story, you know, about what happens when a prophecy does not run its natural course. I see what you just described to me as *something* letting you know that it's there. What it is, I don't know. Don't the le Fay have a family history book? Might be in there."

"Lilly said she has talked to my mom."

"Have you talked to your mom? I mean, since...."

"No. I summoned Lilly both times completely by accident. She was the first and only person I have ever... summoned."

"Was it weird the first time it happened?" he asked.

"Hell yeah. My eyes vibrated. It was bizarre. And scary. Did I mention scary? I don't know if I'll ever get used to that."

He smiled, pushing one of the cups of coffee in my direction.

"Let's do some actual work and find out what Bliss's deal is," he said. "We can figure out that other stuff later."

And we did exactly that. I wasn't sure how long we worked for, but we both sat at our laptops and dug. After what seemed like an eternity, I sighed loudly and pushed my computer away.

"I don't have much. Just this." I turned my laptop, so he could see the screen. Luckily, Bliss hadn't deleted me from her Facebook yet. I searched for any information I could find and spotted a picture of her with a group of girls that were all the same age. It was captioned 'me and my girls'. It looked as if they were at some kind of bonfire. I had thought it was friends from nursing school when I first saw it, and maybe they were at some kind of frat party. But on each of their left forearms was a glyph. It was white, so it was hard to spot, but once you saw it, it was clear as day.

"I don't see it," he said, leaning over and squinting at the screen.

I turned it back around, zoomed in on one, and turned it back to him. "That."

"Huh."

"Exactly. Who the fuck gets matching white glyph tattoos? And a bunch of girls all the same age too? Maybe she's in a cult."

"No. Not a cult. A coven or an Order of some sort. Next time Lilly shows up, show her that. And send it to me."

I sent us both the picture and saved a copy to my computer. I brought up a Google search page, then stopped.

"Hey, if I type occult symbols into a search engine, will I get anything legit?" I asked. "Sorry if it's a dumb question. It's not something I ever thought I would be typing in the Google search bar."

"It's not a dumb question. It's not like there is a secret library with this info that we can access. Some of what's online is truthful, some is misdirection."

"Misdirection?"

"Purposefully left there to distract you from the truth. A common practice among ancient orders."

"Ancient orders? You lost me."

"Order of the Dragon. League of Assassins. That sort of thing."

"A Nine Sisters of Avalon sort of thing?"

"Maybe. We have to locate the glyph."

"Would I also find any useful information about demons?"

"Depends on what religion you subscribe to."

I thumped on my desk in frustration. "Great. How the fuck is anyone supposed to learn anything about this stuff? I never got my letter to Hogwarts. I am totally flying blind, and I don't like it."

He smiled and reached across the table to put his hand on my arm. I smiled back and took a deep breath.

"We'll figure it out. Between all of us, we will find something." He grabbed his phone and started typing something.

"Are you texting Millie?" I had not messaged Millie since yesterday, and I felt bad.

"No. What good is having underlings if you can't put them to work," he said.

I shrugged, grabbing my phone and texting Millie. I started with an apology. That was the most important part. Then I told her about the Bliss cop thing and a white tattoo on her forearm.

"Something else we need to address is the Frankenstein issue," I told him when I put my phone down.

"I know. I don't know where to begin with that one."

"I looked into Nikki and Nicole Frank. Nothing. Her phone number is registered to the Kinkaid group," I began. "I have my Dad's files on the Kinkaid's at home. I will go through them and see if there is anything."

"Maybe Millie will have some insight on that. She does have a web of contacts."

"I thought Lilly was her contact in the Kinkaid organization?" My phone beeped before I could say more. It was Millie, saying that she thought it was about time we spoke to the Fitzpatrick's about this Nikki person.

"What do you know about the Fitzpatrick's?" I asked.

He shrugged. "Not a lot. Why?"

"Millie thinks we should go talk to them about Nikki."

"It's not a bad idea. Tell her we'll meet her there later. You and I can get some dinner or something first."

I smiled. "Are you asking me out on a date?"

"Absolutely," he said with a smile.

I leaned across the desk and grabbed the front of his shirt, pulling him towards me so I could kiss him.

When we broke away, he brushed my hair off my face and behind my ear. His touch was soft and gentle. With my hair colour fading out, my confidence in how good it looked had faded. I would have to fix it soon.

The office phone started to ring. It was Ramona paging me.

"Time to be grown-ups for a bit," I said as we stared into each other's eyes. He smiled, giving me a quick kiss before gathering up his stuff.

"I'll see you later." He winked before he headed out, closing the door behind him.

I grabbed the phone, hoping Ramona wasn't mad it took so long for me to answer.

Time to head back *to reality.*

I straightened up my office before Ramona brought in the new client. I took a quick look in the small mirror I kept in my desk to make sure I looked presentable. My eyes were still puffy from crying last night. I hoped the makeup I had on hid it well.

A thin man in a dark suit came in and sat down across from me. His face was almost gaunt, with so little fat on it that all the sharp angles of his bones stuck out. He looked like he should have been on his way to audition for the *Cryptkeeper*, or one of the Gentlemen from *Buffy the Vampire Slayer*. The small amount of hair that he had on his head was so light I could not tell if it was white or very pale blond.

"Hi, I'm Camille Bishop." I extended my arm out to shake hands. He stared at it, confused for a few moments, before lightly touching his palm to mine. His hand was cold and rubbery, and his skin felt thin.

"Hello, I am Mr. Croft." He sounded as if he was working hard to hide an accent. "I would like you to help me find someone."

"Okay." I grabbed my notepad and started writing. "What's their name?"

"Simone. Simone Gregory," he began.

"What does she look like?"

He reached into his pocket and handed me a crumpled photo. I took a shot of it with my phone and secretly took one of him without him noticing.

The image was of a petite girl in her early to mid-20s, dark curly hair, and big green eyes. She was facing foreword and staring blankly at the camera. It looked like a mugshot.

I wrote down some details of her physical description before asking, "Why are you looking for her?"

"Is that something you need to know? I am paying

you to find her. Is that not the important part?"

Ruh roh. "No. Begging your pardon, I have to make sure that you are not out to hurt her in some fashion. If I found her and you decided to kill her, for example, I would then be an accessory to murder. And I enjoy my freedom. I also value human life."

He studied my face. My Spidey sense was going off so much it was like a shock to my spine. I glanced down at my hands, and there was a small bit of white beginning to swirl up from my ring. I quickly put them on my lap so he couldn't see them.

"Understandable. I apologise if I seem untoward. It is quite embarrassing." Mr. Croft licked his lips. "She is my niece, and she has a horrible affliction. She becomes quite melancholy, and has a tendency to disappear during what her mother calls an 'episode'. This time she has been gone for a fort—two weeks."

"An 'episode'?"

"I believe the clinical term for her affliction is bipolar disorder. She has stopped taking her prescriptions."

I wrote all of that down. "I am not sure how much help I can be, or if this would be more of a job for the police."

"Understandable. I have spoken to the police, on several occasions. Their response was that if we can locate her and she is unstable then they can intervene, but not as it stands."

I wrote that down too. That seemed odd. I would have to check with Kiera. Maybe it was a manpower issue.

"Okay, Mr. Croft. Give me a few days, and I will see if I can locate your niece."

"*See?* I don't understand." He looked confused, his head turning to one side. "I thought that was your job."

I laughed. "I wish it was that simple. Even in the digital age there are no guarantees."

"Oh." He stood and looked around the room, as if confused about what he should do next.

"I'll be in touch," I said, not bothering to stand.

I didn't outright refuse to take his case, but I thought about it. He was too odd not to pay attention to, so I decided to investigate it before I did anything else.

He opened the door, and I was surprised to see Ramona waiting for him in the hallway. Was she listening in? Her eyes widened as she glanced at me, and then she showed Mr. Croft out.

I heard the door outside open and close and quick shuffling as Ramona ran back to my office.

"What the hell was that?" I asked as she shut the door.

"Not sure. He asked for you by name when he called," she began, and a knot formed in my stomach. "I couldn't tell if he was just a weird old man on the phone or what the hell. I should have told him you were called out on an emergency when he arrived."

"It's okay. I dealt with it," I said and smiled, keeping my hands on my lap under my desk.

"He wanted you to locate someone?"

"Yeah. No questions asked. He didn't want to tell me anything, he said he was embarrassed because it's his niece with an 'affliction', but there is clearly more to it. My Spidey sense went off the charts."

"Did you get a picture of him by any chance?"

I smiled at her. "Of course. This is not my first day. After that shit with Jane Lowry and Morris Ludlow, I am not taking any chances."

Ramona sighed. "I don't blame you. That poor girl."

"Yeah, let's hope that's the end of my drama for a while."

"I hope so, too, dear." She gave me her best motherly I-have-faith-in-you smile and left.

I'm happy someone does.

Ted came in about an hour later, and his expression was sour.

"Ruh roh," I said as he sat down. "What happened?"

"I was looking into your grandparents," he stated.

"Grandma Bishop won't like that, but I am curious."

"You're *other* grandparents."

"Oh. *Them*."

"These people just get weirder and weirder. Not only did your grandmother pass recently, but two more family members died also. Your grandmother was not well, so that is explainable. But the others. They were young and youngish. And they're just dead."

"Maybe it was an accident."

He chuckled. "You would think. But I went through corners' reports, police reports, all that. And there is nothing. They died, and no one knows why."

"I will ask Millie and see what I can find out. Maybe she knows something."

"I am going to keep looking, but it's weird. Things that are weird don't sit well with me. It usually means something fishy is going on."

"Great. That's just what I need. More fishy shit. I will ask Millie about it tonight."

"You're going out with her again?"

"Is that a problem?"

"Not at all. I am just surprised."

"Well, it's not just about hanging out with Millie. Her daughter Nya is also there. I like the idea that we could be friends. The cooking is going well too."

He smiled. "I am happy to hear you are moving on and finding new friends."

"What happened with Bliss is not something I did. She's got serious problems that are beyond me. And she's hooked up with Tobias Kinkaid." I shuddered when I said his name. "Whatever Fray is into too. Blah."

"You're not hiding in your bed. I'm pleased."

"When have I ever hid in my bed?" I asked. "Wait, don't answer that. When have I hid in my bed when it wasn't related to Jesse?"

There were several occasions when I had been so torn up over something Jesse had done, I had lain in bed for a few days. Things that I should have left him for, but I didn't. Now when I think about it, I am embarrassed I acted like that.

"Good point. Was there anything useable on Jesse's phone?"

"Not that I could see. But I don't know what Kiera is looking for so there could be. I told her what I could. Which reminds me." I grabbed my phone and started texting. "I need to ask Rollo the name of the bar where he found the phone."

"Kiera should be able to figure some of that out with his phone records," he said.

His phone beeped, he examined it, then headed towards the door.

"Sorry. Duty calls." He waved as he closed the door behind him.

My phone beeped too. It was Rollo, I was surprised he was awake. I almost fell out of my chair when I read the message.

Burnt Offerings. They found Jesse's phone at Burnt Offerings.

What the actual fuck.

10.

The rest of the day seemed to drag on forever. I hadn't texted Kiera to tell her where the phone was found. I was still deciding whether getting brownie points was more important than trying to explain Burnt Offerings.

Kiera is a detective. She probably knows exactly what it is and the basics of what goes on there. Or more. What the fuck do I know?

I didn't see Eric before we left L&B, but I texted him to let him know and for him to give me a heads up when he was coming by. I had butterflies thinking about our first date.

What the hell was I going to wear?

As soon as I got in my room and opened my closet door, I began to panic. After my previous experience with the opposite sex, *boys* you may call them, I felt less than adequate.

Eric was different. Not just because he was magic,

literally and figuratively, he was a full grown *man*. I had zero experience with dating, let alone a man.

Because, to be quite serious, what I had done with Jesse and Fray had not been dating. Jesse and I had basically the human equivalent of a toddler being obsessed with a stuffed animal, where I was the toy, and Fray and I had a bogus teenage make-out session or two that was just sad. Was I prepared for someone like Eric?

My phone beeped as I was digging in my closet. I had settled on blue jeans and a white t-shirt; plain and simple. I freshened up my makeup, hoping that by some miracle it helped me look a little less tired, which was one of the main reasons I wore makeup. Accepting the colour fade for what it was, my hair actually looked okay. I would have to make a plan for hair that was higher maintenance because I was totally not used to it. I ran a brush through my hair and fluffed it a bit. I didn't want to look like I was trying too hard.

I couldn't help but wonder if that was why things with Jesse and Fray were the way they were, because I tried too hard. Because I thought there was something there when there wasn't. They both played the game— Jesse, so someone needed him; and Fray, so he could say he banged every girl he ever wanted. Ever. I chuckled to myself, remembering the shmuck had a permanent reminder of me on his forearm.

That's why you never get tattoo's about partners. It's practically a signal for failure. What a moron.

I checked my phone; it was Eric asking if I was ready.

I grabbed a warm sweater and my winter coat. We were going to meet the Fitzpatrick's afterwards, and I had no idea what we were walking into. I wanted to be prepared if we ended up outside.

Because keeping warm while we meet with a pack of werewolves is my biggest problem.

I tried to remain calm when I went downstairs. Ted and Cuddy were at the kitchen table playing cards. Cuddy looked a lot like Ted; dashing, like a 1940's movie star, but with lighter hair like his mother's. That little boy had a piece of my heart like no one else. And I had to stop calling him a little boy, considering he would be graduating from high school soon.

"Out with Millie again?" Ted asked. The two were playing poker for change. Ted was all smiles, and Cuddy looked unimpressed. Cuddy probably didn't remember when the elder Bishop men used to get together to play poker on Thursday nights, which wasn't a bad thing. It was always a shit show.

"Eric, actually. He needs help with something, asked me to tag along. I'm meeting up with Millie later," I said.

Ted smiled. "Happy to hear you and Eric have hit it off."

"Yeah, I like him." I tried to play it cool and not blush like an idiot, so I opened the fridge to hide my red face.

"Well, tell him I said hello," Ted said when he heard my phone beep. He slammed his hand of cards on the table and began to laugh hysterically. Cuddy looked super confused.

I chuckled. "Try not to break Cuddy before I get back."

They both waved as I put on my coat and left. I tried hard not to puke on the porch as I headed to Eric's car parked on the curb out front.

"Hey," he said with a smile. "You look beautiful."

"Thanks. Heads up. If Ted asks, I had to help you with something, so you picked me up." I reached out and grabbed his hand, kissing his knuckles. "Thanks for not hating me."

He kissed my hand, and my heart fluttered. "We're good. I get it. I have to keep in mind that you haven't known about all this your whole life."

"Yeah, it's a *fucking lot.*"

"Don't worry about that now. Let's try to have a drama-free evening before we go see the Fitzpatrick's." He kissed my hand again, then started the car and drove off.

"So what am I walking into with this Fitzpatrick thing?"

"What do you mean?"

"It's cold in the forest this time of year."

He laughed. "Where exactly is this forest you speak of? You remember we live in Toronto, right? Like there would be werewolves running loose in High Park?"

"Don't laugh at me. I'm serious. I don't want to look like an idiot. I'm a PI. Not knowing what I am getting into could make me break out in hives."

"We can talk about it over dinner. But no, we will not be out in a forest. It won't be much different than the poker games. Only in my experience, with werewolves, they're very...friendly."

"What do you mean 'friendly'?"

"They like to touch hands, hug. That sort of thing. They are very physical and affectionate, which can be off putting for people who don't like to be touched. I had heard stories that they sleep in piles like puppies, but I don't know for sure."

"Ask Millie. I think she was boning Liam Fitzpatrick. She may still be, I'm not sure. She gets all giggly and red faced when you mention his name."

He laughed. I wanted to tell him I wasn't kidding, but he parked in front of a house and turned off the car. I had lost track of how long we were driving.

When I looked out the window, we were on a quiet street in front of a row of townhouses. The lawns had a light dusting of snow, but the neighbourhood looked quaint and well kept.

"This is your place?" I asked, pointing up at the townhouse. It had a cute cobblestone walkway leading up to a small patio with two chairs out front of a big window. I couldn't see anything inside because the lights were off. It was far quainter than I expected.

"Yep. It's all mine. Just me here." He got out of the car, ran around, and opened my door for me. When I stepped outside, he took me into his arms and kissed me.

He smiled at me when we separated. "Hi."

I couldn't help but smile back. "Hi."

I hugged him tightly, maybe a little longer than I

should have.

"I'm sorry I'm such a shmuck," I said, my face nuzzling his neck.

"Don't be." He took my hand and led me towards the front door.

The townhouse was bigger than I expected. An open entryway branched off to a small black and white kitchen to the left, the stairs to the upper level to the right, and it ended at an open living room. Another flight of stairs under the first one led to a basement.

The living room was decorated in taupe and light brown, with a bleached white wood floor. One wall was lined with bookshelves, another had a large tv. An overstuffed couch and love seat were very inviting.

He motioned for me to sit down after he took my coat. "Would you like anything to drink?"

"You got any hard liquor?" I asked.

"No. Do you think it's a good idea to go to the Fitzpatrick's drunk?"

"I wasn't going to get *drunk*. I just need something to take the edge off. I am terrified."

"They are probably more scared of you than you are of them."

I laughed a little too loud. "Right. Because I'm *so scary*."

"Says the girl with the *white hands*." He gestured towards me.

Because we were in his place I figured I didn't need the gloves, but when I looked at my hands they were bright white. The glow they radiated when they were full blown *Blanchmains* was unsettling to me, I can't imagine how they looked to other people.

"Yeah, I don't get it. I think they have, like, magic radar. Or they really like you. Because they get super white when you are around."

He smiled. "They like me?"

"Well, yes. What else would you call it?" I stared down at my hands as he came over to me and sat down on the couch, pulling me into his arms. I kept my hands bundled in my lap as we kissed.

"What's wrong?" he asked.

"I'm scared. I don't know what will happen if my bare hand touches your cheek when they look like this." I smiled awkwardly at him. "Now I know what Rogue feels like."

"Who?"

"From the X-Men. She touches people, and they wither and die."

"The one with the white streak in her hair?"

"I'm impressed you got that," I began, but I stopped mid sentence as he took my hand in his. Our skin touched, and his hands were warm and felt strong.

"We have touched hands many times, Camille," he said. "Rogue couldn't even do that."

"Yes, except I don't think I have touched your face or close to your heart. That may be different. I don't get how all this works."

He took my hand and placed it over his heart. I tried to pull back before my hand made contact, but he held on. When my palm finally touched his chest, nothing happened.

"I wonder if the X-Men creator based Rogue's powers on *Blanchmains*," I said breathlessly.

"See? Nothing. It doesn't work with touch unless you make it. Our sorts of powers don't work unless you're actually trying," he replied.

I focused my thoughts and began to lift his coffee table a foot off the ground and put it down, smiling proudly.

He laughed. "Yes, I mean like that. I didn't know *Blanchmains* had telekinesis."

"It's not super useful yet. It's going to be hysterical to fuck with my family at parties and Christmas."

He pulled me to him and kissed me again. This time, I gently touched his face with both my hands. His skin was warm, and his stubble made the tips of my fingers tingle.

"We should eat," he said with a smile.

"We should?"

"Is that a question?"

"I can think of a few other things we could do that are *far* more fun than eating."

He laughed. "Why, Miss Bishop. If I didn't know better, I would think you were trying to seduce me."

"Is it working?"

He laughed again. "In time, sweetheart. We will get to all that in time. When we have no obligations, and there are no interruptions. Now, let me fix us some dinner."

"There will always be something. It seems like lately there is always something. As soon as I reconnected with Bliss again, it's like a fucking shit cloud. I can't believe I didn't see it sooner. How could I not know she was lying to me?"

"That reminds me." He got up and walked over to his bookshelf. He pulled out a few books so thick they looked like cement blocks. The way he flipped through the pages, I assumed they were some type of encyclopaedia, casually skipping large sections like one would skip unnecessary letter sections. Two books did not have what he was looking for, but halfway through the third, he stopped and laid the book out flat.

"Bring me the photo of Bliss and her 'classmates'," he said without looking up. I grabbed my phone and brought it to him. He zoomed in on the glyph in the photo and laid it beside the book.

Sure enough, the same glyph was on the page.

"That's what I thought. She's a *bruja*. And not just an ordinary *bruja*." He pushed the book in my direction.

I groaned loudly and threw my hands in the air. "Great! Fan-fucking-tastic. Another magical thingy I don't know how to deal with. This is fantastic!"

"Do you want to read the page?"

"Just give me the Coles notes version. My crap-dealing level has about reached its limit."

"They do everything in the name of a 'reina', a queen. They call themselves 'oscuro', which basically means dark.

They are handmaidens to this queen."

"*Bruja* handmaidens. Witch handmaidens. Are you serious?"

"Does she know what you are?"

"Yes. I figured she didn't get it, so I paraphrased. She was there when I killed some le Fay relatives. Long story. She saw me use my powers."

"And she did not try to kill you? Hmm."

"Not yet. Is that all you got? Hmm?"

He pulled me to him and hugged me. "They don't see you as a threat. That's good. I assume you were a gateway."

"Gateway to what?"

"The bigger prize. The only reason an Oscuro bruja would be that close to a Kinkaid is if their Queen wants blood. Which you want to be as far away from as possible. So while you may be upset about what happened, in the long run karma is going to come back and bite her in the ass. Bliss is on a mission that will either end in her destruction or a full blown war, and we need to stay out of it."

I wasn't sure if he thought that would make me feel better, knowing that if Bliss had played me—because in a way she had no choice—it would somehow make it hurt less. Knowing that her lies will eventually come back to haunt her helped a little.

"This is all too fucky for my brain to take. Fray helped create the damn virus, Bliss is a witch henchwoman, and Jesse's phone was found in a garbage can outside Burnt

Offerings—wait. How are siblings affected by the bruja thing?"

"What do you mean?"

"Bliss had a brother named Bucky. Lucia Kinkaid had him beaten to death. He was friends with Jesse and went missing right around when Jesse died. And Jesse's phone was at Burnt Offerings."

"Why would Lucia have Bliss's brother beaten to death?"

"Bliss claimed that Lucia was trying to make a point. That Bliss belonged to her and her brothers. But Bliss shot her in the head and disposed of her body. That's why I thought she had been kidnapped, and why I was so frantic to find her. I thought they were going to kill her for what she did to Lucia, and then come for me." The realization of what I had just confessed hit me hard. It felt good to admit the truth to someone."Oops. Yeah, I was there when Bliss killed Lucia. But you can't tell *anyone*. About me or Lucia being dead. Millie knows, but that's it."

He hugged me tighter. "Don't worry. I won't tell anyone. I will protect you when or if the time comes."

We stood there for a few minutes,and he just held me in his arms. I took a deep breath and focused on the moment.

"I have to let go before I don't want to anymore. We need to eat before we go." He kissed my head and released me. I plopped down on his couch as he disappeared into his kitchen.

Eric made this incredible pasta dish with shrimp that looked like a picture from a cookbook. He smiled shyly at my compliments, his eyes sparkling with pride. I insisted he let me clean up, so I washed dishes as he dried and put them away.

"So do you want to fool around before we go?" I asked, poking him in the side and wiggling my eyebrows at him.

He kissed me on the cheek. "We don't have enough time."

"Oh? But we don't have to be there for a couple of hours."

"Remember what I told you before about dealing with men and not boys?"

"Yeah?"

"Well," he brushed my hair behind my ear and kissed my neck. "Men don't work well with time constraints. When it's finally time for us to be together, I want to take my time."

He ran his finger down my neck and along my throat. "I want to memorize every inch of you. And I want *you* to remember me."

My face flushed, and I giggled like a toddler. His smile made it hard to keep my hands off of him. I could have sworn my body turned into melted butter.

"We gotta go. We don't want to be late," he said.

Neither of us moved though, and we stared into each other's eyes. I debated blowing off the whole thing and locking us in his bedroom. If I didn't need to find Bliss, why the fuck were we even going?

"Nikki," he told me.

"Huh?" I asked.

"We're going because of Nikki Frank," he continued.

"Did you just read my mind?"

He laughed. "No. But I was reminding myself, so I figured you needed the reminder too."

"Right. Before we go, we should take a quick photo of that page you showed me in the book. That way we can show it to Millie and Nya."

He kissed me on the cheek. "Absolutely. Now, let's go before I change my mind."

We drove for longer than I expected, to the north part of the city close to the Credit Valley River. On both sides of the road there were lots of big healthy trees, immaculate lawns, and well-groomed houses that should be in magazines. In a small parking lot just outside a wooded park area was Millie's SUV. Eric parked beside her. When we got out of the car, the hairs on my arms immediately stood up. Energy vibrated off me like static electricity. I could smell the water and the trees, and something else that I didn't understand.

Millie was waiting outside her vehicle bundled up in her winter coat. Nya wasn't with her. I zipped my coat up and put on my gloves. Eric had on a hoodie and a leather jacket. I was colder just looking at him.

"Why are we out here?" I asked her.

She pointed into the wooded area, where the glow of a fire could be seen off in the distance.

"This is how they do things. If we want to talk to the whole pack at once, this is the easiest way to do it," she replied.

My nerves went into hyper drive. "The whole pack? You didn't tell me the whole pack would be here. And we're welcome?"

"Yes, and you have nothing to worry about. You don't need to hide here either. You can take your gloves off if you want."

I shrugged. "It's cold. I'm good with my gloves on. And, of course, I am going to be worried. That's kind of my thing."

Millie and I linked arms, then the three of us headed off into the woods side by side. My emotions were so mixed, ranging from scared shitless to amused that we were walking into Narnia to see some wolves.

"Have you been here before?" I asked Eric.

"Yes, but not for a while. Liam and I are friendly though," he replied.

"Hopefully not friendly like he and Millie are friendly," I joked, poking Millie's arm. She blushed so hard I could see how red her face was even in the darkness.

"I'm kidding!" I exclaimed. Thankfully, Millie laughed. I felt Eric's body tense beside me.

"Sorry. I don't think we've met. I'm socially awkward Camille who makes bad jokes that make people uncomfortable," I said to him with a grin. "I may do that again tonight, so please feel free to magic it out of me, if you can."

He chuckled. "I wish it worked that way. Don't worry, you'll be fine."

We stepped out into an opening. It was a nice family barbeque with a roaring fire and heat lamps surrounding the clearing. Picnic tables were spaced out so there was an empty space in the middle, where someone could stand and talk to the whole group if necessary. All eyes turned to us, and the noise went down. I felt like a deer caught in headlights.

Appropriate, considering the circumstances.

Liam appeared from in the crowd, and Millie smiled. He looked happy to see us. Power radiated off of him like steam does from hot food. His body seemed fluid when he moved, like he wasn't built to stand still.

"Welcome! It's nice to see you all again," Liam said. He had on a pair of dark jeans, a black hoodie and leather jacket overtop, and the type of boots that men usually wear when they work in construction. He seemed so calm and at ease, but had a presence that commanded attention.

I giggled awkwardly and tried to smile, even though I wanted to run. Why was I so scared? This was the place I should be the least afraid. Liam had been nothing but nice to me. The others smiled at us, floating around like extras in a movie. I made an effort to look and smile at every one of them. There were only five others that I could see, maybe they all didn't come out. Or they were staying back in the shadows until they decided if we were okay, which was understandable. Part of me wanted to do the same thing. We were the invaders in their space. They could handle the situation however they wanted as long as we didn't get hurt.

"Thanks for inviting us," Millie replied, and lead us to a nearby bench. "Seems like we have a lot to talk about."

"Yes, we do," Liam began, turning to me. "I think to fully get an idea of what is happening, we need *everyone* to be here."

I stared blankly at him. "Nya needs to be here?"

"No, Camille. He means Lilly," Millie told me. I stared at her, completely dumbfounded. Was this why they had made the circle in the middle of the picnic tables? They didn't need room for someone to speak, they wanted to parade around the freak like I was in a side show.

I turned to Eric. "Did you know about this?"

"She knows more about Nikki than anyone. It makes sense." He didn't look me in the eye when he replied.

"Were you trying to butter me up so I would do this? I told you both now—"

"No. You know as well as I do that we are flying blind. We *need* to know what we are dealing with, and Lilly knows things we don't." Eric grabbed my hand, now making sure he made eye contact.

I sighed. "I have never summoned someone on purpose before. I don't even know if I can."

Liam eyed me carefully. He seemed confused, but his expression remained blank. It was easy to assume that he didn't know as much about me as I had thought.

"Just try to do what you did before," Eric said quietly. "Don't overthink it. Maybe it will just happen."

"Okay." I took a deep breath and tried to push back my nervousness. I thought about Lilly, about her pretty long hair. I wondered if her name was actually Tiger Lilly. My power swirled around inside me, pushing itself out to my edges.

My vision went milky, and my eyes shook. The feeling was so nauseating that I wanted to vomit. I tried to breathe through it, pushing back that beautiful dinner that Eric made before it made a second appearance. I squeezed Eric's hand as my stomach flip flopped, and I blinked a few times. The power pushed, and I felt like I was going to come apart at the seams.

"What. The. *Fuck*!" Lilly snapped. I looked up and saw her standing by one of the heat lamps. All pain and feelings of upchucking went away when I saw her.

"I'm sorry. I had to. They want to talk about Nikki," I said to her. No one asked who I was talking to, or said anything for that matter.

"Since when are you someone's bitch? That doesn't look good on you, *Blanchmains,* to be taking orders this early on in your career. What the fuck do you want to know about Nikki?"

"We have to stop her. We have to stop the virus."

Lilly laughed. "Being the prophecy girl doesn't make you smart, does it? You can't do shit, so don't fucking bother."

"She says we can't do shit about the virus," I told

the group, but I kept my eyes on Lilly. I was worried if I looked away now all the bad I had felt when summoning her would come back.

She turned her head and stared at something beside her. The darkness began to ripple like water. Fear hit me like a punch in the face, and something inside me said it was time to go. Like right now.

She laughed. "I fucking knew it!"

"Knew what? What are you looking at?" My mouth went dry. "What is that?"

"Me," a deep female voice said, and I jumped. "I am here now, *Blanchmains*. But I have no form, so you cannot see me. Could you help me find a form?"

"I don't understand," I said quietly. The nervousness I'd already had shook hands with this new bit of fear and began to tap dance on my stomach.

"What is it, Camille?" Eric asked quietly.

"Tell him!" Lilly exclaimed. "Tell them all *I was right about the fucking demon*!"

"They did not tell you, *Blanchmains*?" it said. I could tell it was laughing at me.

Stupid girl.

"What do you want?" I asked.

"I want to be like you. I want a form," it continued. "I could join yours, or perhaps the Merlin. No! No. That young man you live with, or your guardian perhaps?"

"*Don't you touch them!*" I screamed at it. Eric's body tensed, and the energy around us shifted. My anger took over, and I was relieved. In this situation, fear wouldn't do me any good. I would set the entire world on fire before I let this thing touch my family.

"You have bigger worries than Frankenstein now, bitch!" Lilly cackled. "You better find this fucker a body *and quick!*"

"Will you find me a form, *Blanchmains*? If you find me a form, I will not bother your loved ones." The demon cooed like it was trying to coax a small child into getting into its creepy van. "But if you don't, I will start with your guardian and his son."

"I will find you a form. Just leave them alone," I told it.

"No…no," Millie said from beside me, but I ignored her.

"Of course. Summon me when it is time," it said.

"What is your name?" I asked.

"*Noirmains*, of course." It laughed. Then it was gone.

"Tell me how to find Nikki," I snapped at Lilly. Anger was now at home in my body. I had no room for any other emotion.

"You can't be that dumb. *The virus is already out in the world.* Focus on more important things. Like *that* demon," she told me sharply, then completely vanished.

"What just happened?" Eric asked when I turned back to him.

"She made a deal with a demon." Millie didn't bother hiding her disappointment.

"It would have gone after Ted and Cuddy. I had no choice." I couldn't fight back my tears. "Lilly said going after Nikki is a waste of time. The virus is already out in the world. And that I have more important issues. I am inclined to agree considering she hasn't been wrong before."

"Why would the demon go after Ted and Cuddy?" Eric asked.

"It wants a form. It threatened Ted. And Cuddy."

"Making promises to—"

"And you. It threatened you too."

He squeezed my hand and said nothing. I hoped that he understood. I would have to find a way to make Millie understand.

"Why would Lilly not be afraid?" I asked, turning to him and wiping my tears. "How could she be standing that close to a demon and not be afraid?"

My phone started vibrating in my purse. I ignored it. But then it vibrated again. And again. And again. I ignored it while I waited for someone to answer me, my purse made an odd humming noise like a swarm of bees approaching. With that amount of noise someone must have called multiple times.

I got fed up and put my purse on my lap and dug around for my phone.

"Everything good?" Eric asked.

"Someone keeps calling. It must be important." I finally found my phone and answered it without looking at the number, "Hello?"

"Yo, Camille. You can't answer your phone?" Q's voice sounded panicked. She rarely called me by my first name so I knew it was serious.

"Sorry. Long story. What's up?"

"Lemme's gone."

"Gone? What do you mean, gone?"

"Gone as in cannot be located. Gone as in disappeared, vanished, not present. Last I heard was that contact you had wanted to meet her about some samples and then, poof."

"Contact?" *Oh my God*.

"You know, the contact you had sending her samples. Not your cousin, the other one. She called, wanted to meet her. Poof."

"Alright, I'm on—"

"*I'm not done*," Q growled. "Her lab is on fire, Camille."

"*What!*"

"I am standing outside the building right now. The entire floor that the lab was on is on fire. They evacuated the goddamn building."

"Did you call Ted?"

"Bitch, are you stupid? This is on *you*. Find my friend! Please."

"I will, Q. I will find *our* friend. I promise," I said, and she hung up.

"We have a problem. A big problem," I began, loud enough that they could all hear. "Someone snatched one of my techs and torched a U of T lab, all because she was analysing the virus."

"Is it Q?" Eric asked.

"No, the other girl, Lemme." I continued, "I have to go and get her. Someone else can't die because of me."

"How do we find her?" Millie asked.

"Q said the last she heard from Lemme was my contact wanted to meet her with samples for testing. That contact being Bliss. Bliss told me that she was an undercover cop, and she would get her friend in the police lab to send my friend samples infected with the virus. I'm going to try her old number." I tried Bliss's number from my phone, and it rang and rang. "I don't know what to do."

"Why would she do that to your tech?" Liam asked. "Why would she care about the virus?"

"She wouldn't. But Tobias Kinkaid would. Nikki works for the Kinkaid's."

My phone started vibrating again, this time from an unknown number. Hoping it was Bliss, I answered it quickly.

I put the phone on speaker. "Hello?"

"Hey there, Camille. This is Nikki. I got your number from Fray, I'm sure you don't mind as I have something you may want." Nikki's voice was way too calm and casual.

"Oh? What's that?" I asked. My hands started turning white, flowing up to my elbows. They glowed eerily. My anger seemed to stay confined to my hands, which was good for the moment. Letting her know that she got to me would give her the upper hand, and she already had Lemme. I wouldn't give her more.

"U of T had quite an amazing set up. Not as great as mine though. You should come see it sometime."

"If you hurt her..."

"Oh, I have no intention of hurting her. Bliss might, but that's a whole other story."

"What do you want?"

"I want you to meet me. Do that, and I will give you back your friend in one piece. With all that business with Fray, I sort of feel like we got off on the wrong foot."

"Where and when?" I immediately thought of Lilly, willing her to appear, and she did. Summoning her didn't hurt this time.

"I will text you an address. Meet me in one hour," she hung up without saying goodbye.

"Was that Nikki?" Lilly asked, laughing. "Oh, you fucked now!"

"She has my tech. I'm not letting anything happen to her, Lilly." I stood up and walked over to the ghost. "Tell me something so I am not flying blind here."

"Does Bliss know the truth about you?" Lilly asked.

"Sort of, but I got some shit on her. She's a *bruja*, loyal to a queen or some shit."

Lilly's mouth hung open and she stared at me. "Fuck off. Are you serious?"

"Absolutely. You had no idea, did you?" I took out my phone and showed Lilly the glyph. "This is on her arm. Look familiar?"

"Son of a bitch!" she yelled. "I can't believe she got passed me! I can't believe she got passed any of Tobias's peeps...dude, that's your ace in the hole. *That* is your trump card. Whatever they have on you does not mean shit."

"She had no idea?" Millie asked.

"Nope. And she seems to think that will help us." My phone vibrated, it was a text from the unknown number. Sure enough, it was an address downtown, not far from Fray's loft.

I turned back to the group. "So, are any of you coming or am I calling a cab? Because I have to go. Like now."

They all hesitated for a moment, and I turned to Liam. "Look, I get it if you all don't want to come. You and your pack, you don't know me. I could be coocoo for Coco Puffs. All you know is this," I waved my glowing white hand at them, "and that says nothing about me as a person. But they have an innocent girl, who knows fuck all of this life, and I have to go and get her. They did this to her because of me, and I can't do nothing. And my other tech girl will kill me. Then tell my uncle. Shit just goes south from there, and it's a bad scene for everyone. I have to go."

I turned and trampled back through the woods, not paying attention to make sure I didn't trip. I didn't wait to see if anyone was coming. I didn't think anyone would come and that was fine. I had already gotten enough people hurt.

Maybe, just maybe, that apologetic text was from Bliss, and this is part of an elaborate plan.

You're a moron.

Eric and Millie caught up to me by the time I got back

to the vehicles. Liam Fitzpatrick was not far behind.

"Liam and I will take my vehicle and meet you there. What's the address?" I opened the text and read the location out to her.

"We have an hour."

"Are you prepared for this to go south?" Liam asked, and I started laughing hysterically.

"What's so funny?" he asked.

"Sorry! I have just been getting asked that question *a lot* lately," I said. "But yes, I am prepared. And I will keep my gloves on unless it's absolutely necessary. Does this mean you're choosing a side?"

He laughed. "I'm on the side I am always on, sweetheart. *Mine.*"

I turned to Eric, smiling at him, and softly touched his cheek. He looked down at me, a slight twinkle in his eye.

"You don't have to do this," I said.

He smiled, taking my hand. "Yes, I do. Now let's go get her. I have a feeling pissing Q off is a *very* bad idea."

11.

Silence filled the car as we drove. I spent most of the time deciding what lengths I was willing to go to to get Lemme back.

Whatever it takes.

It didn't surprise me when we pulled up in front of a warehouse in midtown. It was still clearly operational, with boxes stacked around the loading dock in the back and skids stacked off near garbage bins. I could have thrown a rock and hit Fray's building. I laughed to myself.

"What's funny?" Eric asked me as he parked. I grabbed the front of his shirt and pulled him to me, kissing him. His warmth gave me energy and strength.

"Nothing. Are we good?" I asked.

"Absolutely. Are you ready for what might happen in there?"

"Are you? I have done this a few times now. It's kinda becoming my thing."

"Does that bother you at all?"

"It can't. I spent a lot of time being powerless, and feeling like I could do fuck all about what was going on in my life. Now, it's different. *Now,* I can protect myself and my loved ones. This is me waving my middle fingers in the air screaming 'Fuck the Free World'."

"What's that from?"

"*8 Mile*. The movie with Eminem? You haven't seen it?"

"No, I haven't."

"Well, I know what our first movie date is then."

He rolled his eyes. "Anyways, are you ready to face Bliss again?"

"Most definitely. I just have to get her to use her powers. Easy peasy."

"Might not be as simple as you think. She has gone to great lengths to hide herself."

"I just have to piss her off bad enough. You haven't spent enough time around me to fully get that I'm *really* good at pissing people off. Don't forget, I also know that she killed Lucia Kinkaid."

"But that would incriminate you too."

I shrugged. "Might be worth it. And if they want to come at me for it, let them come. Now, let's go before I chicken out."

Time to put my big girl pants on.

Marcus Kinkaid stood guard at the door, looking like an angry gargoyle in a t-shirt he stole from a six-year-old. This was too easy.

"Evening, crypt keeper," I said happily to him. "Your vamp tramp stole something of mine, and I am here to get it back."

Marcus looked behind me. His pupils dilated, and his neck muscles tensed. He did a good job trying to hide his irritation, but I was standing too close to him. He vibrated with so much energy, I was surprised it didn't knock me over. His attempt to look intimidating, with his melted looking skin and snaggle tooth snarl, was cartoonish.

"You good there, Marcus?" I asked, still smiling and ignoring him overlooking me. "Hope you don't mind I brought my people. Can't be too careful these days."

I wasn't sure if it was Liam or Eric, or even Millie, causing him to react like that, and it didn't matter. I wanted to make him uncomfortable. *Them* uncomfortable. I was tired of the nonsense. They needed to know that they aren't the big bad wolf. Ignoring me as a potential threat was a good thing.

"Can you take us to Nikki? I am on a schedule here," I pointed behind him into the building. "C'mon now, fuckboy. Time to do your job."

He laughed and said nothing, just turned around and went inside.

As we followed him, Eric whispered sharply, "Are you trying to pick a fight before we even get in the door?"

"Trust me. I have a plan," I replied.

Marcus escorted us to a large room near the back. It was dirty, with broken bits of wood and other things scattered around. They had done a good job of making this warehouse look like it was still in use from the outside, but from the broken bits of glass and stained concrete I could tell it was just a facade. Light crept in from a crack somewhere on the ceiling, illuminating this spot on the ground that looked oddly enough like dried blood. We were in the main area where most of the work would have been done, which they had turned into some sort of meeting room.

Bliss had Lemme by the arm, a big knife in her free hand. It looked like a hunting knife, with a large serrated blade and a handle that was enormous in Bliss's small hand. Lemme seemed more annoyed than scared, which was a good thing. Fear would not help us.

Tobias sat off to one side, sipping from a disposable coffee cup. He smiled and waved like an idiot when he saw me. What did she see in him? His scrawny little face reminded me of a weasel, only weasel's are cuter.

"Camille! At last we finally meet!" a female voice exclaimed from the back of the room. A girl appeared, a blonde in her mid-20s with sharp angular features and grinning like a moron.

Keep up the attitude, dummy. Your friend is in trouble.

"You alright, Lemme? These fuckboys treating you okay?" I asked, gesturing towards the arm Bliss was holding. "Don't worry, we'll get you tested for super syphilis later."

"Fuck you," Bliss snarled.

I laughed. "Naw, I'm good. Vamp tramp is not my thing."

I flicked my wrist, twisting a coil of energy out to yank on her hair. She growled, flicking her hair back and pulling Lemme closer to her. This would either work or make things really bad, really fast. I was willing to roll the dice if it helped me get Lemme out unharmed.

"Hey, back over here! I am the one you need to talk to." Nikki waved in my direction. "I heard you're looking for friends."

"Do you have something for me now, Blanchmains*?"* The demon's voice whispered in my head. A cold breeze blew on my neck, as if the demon was standing behind me whispering in my ear.

"Is that not true?" Nikki asked. "Are you not desperate for friends? Because I think we can be friends. I think it could be mutually beneficial for both of us."

I flicked my wrist again, this time using the coil to push into Bliss and causing her to stumble. She looked a little annoyed, so I did it again and pulled her hair at the same time. Tobias watched her in confusion. I had wondered if maybe he knew what she was and just never told anyone, but the look on his face said otherwise.

I almost didn't want Bliss to fall for it. All it did was make me right, and I still—in some small part—didn't want to be right. I wanted to believe in who I thought Bliss was. No matter how hard I tried to shut up the naive little fuck in my head I couldn't.

"I often need someone to find things for me, whether it be a person or a thing. That is what you do, right?" Nikki continued. "And I wanted to ask, what happened with you and Fray? I called him a few days ago, and he was making plans to leave the country."

I laughed a little harder than I should have. Knowing you were successful when you actively tried to scare someone was amazing.

Good. Fuck him.

"I was honest with him. I guess he didn't like it. Some people just can't deal with honesty, right Bliss?" I turned my eyes to my former friend, tormenting her again with a magical poke. "Lord knows how some people would feel if they found out the *real truth*, right?"

Nikki waved like she was shooing away a fly. "No matter, he was of no use anymore. Not just as a lackey, but as a boy toy. Am I right?"

"I wouldn't know. I never slept with him."

"Really? Well, trust me when I say, you're not missing much."

"That's all fine and dandy, but can we get down to business? I'd like my friend back."

"Do you mean Bliss?"

I hesitated, then laughed. I pushed at Bliss again, this time almost knocking her over. I was trying to loosen her grip on Lemme. As I lifted my hand up and down, my power smacked her face like I was slapping her.

While holding on to Lemme with one hand, she threw the knife high into the air and formed this glowing orb in her hand. It shot out of her palm at me, and I ducked out of the way, pushing Eric behind me. It bounced off a protective wall that appeared in front of us.

When I looked back, Bliss had caught the knife, and the glyph on her arm was glowing. It wasn't quite glowing like my hands did, but enough that it was noticeable. Like a digital watch lighting up with the time,

Cool trick. Wish she could have taught me that.

"No. I mean the girl you kidnapped," I told Nikki. I took a breath in and out, standing up a little straighter.

Tobias was on his feet and heading towards Bliss. He grabbed her arm, where the mark was, looking from it to her. Bliss's expression soured when she realized what she had done. What I made her do.

Gotcha.

"You *liar!*" he yelled. He went to grab Bliss by the throat, and before he could, she stuck the knife into Lemme's side.

I screamed, and the room started to shake. A dark shape appeared in my peripheral vision, and I ignored it; I was not concerned with the damn demon at the moment. I focused on making the biggest, strongest thread that I could and attaching it to Bliss. Lemme would not die.

"*Got one for you,*" I said to the demon, in my mind. I could feel its excitement building as if it was my own.

The knife clattered to the floor and Lemme clutched her wound, blood seeped out between her entwined fingers.

The thread took a second before it finally attached, and I sensed every little piece as it latched onto Bliss. She turned to me, her eyes filled with horror as Tobias grabbed her throat and began to squeeze. I didn't know if she was more afraid of me or of Tobias.

Bliss let go of Lemme, who stumbled while she clutched her side. I used my powers to pull Lemme to us. Liam and Millie grabbed her when she fell at our feet.

"No! No! No!" Nikki screamed, stomping her feet like a child. "This is not supposed to happen this way! *We* need *her*! Grandfather said—"

"Do you understand what she is?" Tobias snapped at Nikki. I caught a glimpse of his face, and his fangs. He held Bliss up by the wrist and dangled her in front of Nikki, reminding her who the she was he spoke of.

"If it makes you feel any better she lied to me too, Tobias," I called out to him. I knew it probably wasn't helpful, but I didn't care. If I were him, I would want to know.

He squeezed Bliss's neck a little tighter, and the demon spoke to me again.

I like her.

My conscience told me that this was a bad idea. That I would regret this later. But in that split second, my anger bitch slapped my conscience out of the way.

If I had to choose between Bliss and my family, I would choose my family. *Every single time.* This thing had threatened them. And Eric. She had hurt me. Now it was her turn to hurt. After what she had done to Lemme, this was nothing.

"*Get ready. Your time is now,*" I told the demon, then I twisted and turned Bliss's thread.

Her face went white as a sheet. Her irises split in two for a second, then reconnected. She blinked, and then there was something else there. Her body twitched like she was coughing, and I saw her shadow darken. Bliss's face turned back to me and smiled a menacing grin, sending shivers down my spine. There was a coldness, a deeply consuming darkness that filled her eyes, and it was frightening. I had never seen anything like that.

I was pretty confident that no one saw it but me. Tobias was yelling at her, and then she grabbed him by the wrist, and he stopped. She said something I couldn't hear, and he let her go. But was it Bliss or her new dark passenger?

I could use this to our advantage. Someone or something on the inside that owes me a favour.

"What the *hell* are you?!" Nikki yelled at me.

I took a deep breath, and the room calmed down. My power shifted, the energy dying down as my emotions settled. Liam and Millie picked up Lemme. They were surprisingly calm, considering she was bleeding.

I couldn't think about that now. I wasn't done yet.

"It's not deep," Liam said quietly. "We'll take her to my doctor. She will be fine."

"Answer me bitch!" Nikki screamed at me as she stepped towards us. I turned to her, and she stopped. Every part of her frozen except her head. Just like I had done to her precious Fray, she was contained within a strangle hold of my powers.

I sighed and rolled my eyes. I debated taking my

gloves off and showing her exactly who I was, but didn't. Tobias was still in the room, and Marcus was around, probably hiding in a corner with the other rats. I wasn't ready to throw down just yet. My secret was more important than my anger.

"My name is Camille Bishop. I might be just like you. Only, I'm not. I am a le Fay. I am a descendant of the Nine Sisters of Avalon. And I am sick and fucking tired of people thinking they can kick me around," I growled as I stepped closer to her and pointed a gloved finger in her face. "No, I don't want to be your *friend*, you crazy bitch. I want you and whatever the fuck this is," I gestured widely at the room, "to leave me and my people alone. Plain and simple. Can you do that? Or do I have to be honest with *you* like I was honest with Fray?"

I tilted my head to one side, watching her face as what I said went through her mind. She had a thin nose that was a little pointy, but was small enough to look delicate. Her icy blue eyes were sharp and penetrating.

"Tell me, Nikki," I began, getting about a foot away from her. "This Frankenstein thing, is it true?"

She laughed. "Are you a believer, Camille?"

"Answer the question."

"Yes."

"Why do you work for the Kinkaid's? You could be—"

"Not *for*," she snapped. "*With*. Don't get it twisted."

"Sorry. *With*. Why do you work *with* the Kinkaid's? Why did you make the virus? Do you understand what you have done?"

"Why? You got the virus?" she asked. She smiled, making her thin lips almost disappear.

"No. I got the antidote from Lilly Darling."

"Oh yeah? Where is the little traitor anyway?"

"You haven't heard? She's dead."

Nikki snorted. "Not a surprise. She was weak."

I twisted my wrist, and the hold I had squeezed like a vice grip around her. Her eyes got big, and her face turned red.

"Stop dodging the question. Why did you make the virus?"

"To make a better breed of human. To weed out the weak. The vampires were the original carriers, and then it got passed on. Anyone else, if they survive, is strong enough to live in the new world we intend on creating."

"Who is *we*? You and the Kinkaid's? You know they will throw you under the bus if they need to, right?"

She laughed again. "They're funding. A means to an end. When we find the immortals, it won't matter anymore."

I paused, thinking so hard about the stupid shit she just babbled that it made me squint.

"That's so fucky I can't even process it." I turned to Eric. "Are you hearing this shit? Does any of it make sense to you?"

"Unfortunately." He walked up from behind me and took my hand. "What do you want to do?" he asked.

I made another thread, this one not as thick as the one I did for Bliss, and attached it to Nikki.

I held up my hands so she could see them, then I tugged gently on her thread. Not hard enough to kill her, but she felt it. I could tell by the look on her face.

Tobias stood off to the side, holding Bliss by the wrist. I glanced briefly at them, and the demon smiled at me from Bliss's face. I tried not to cringe.

Ruh roh.

"As you can see, I can fuck you up pretty bad without touching you. So I am going to tell you now, and only once. You and your people will leave me and mine alone. Understand?" I let her go, and she dropped to the ground, coughing. "The only reason you are not dead right now is because you did not hurt Lemme. You said you wouldn't. And you kept your word."

I approached her and crouched down to look in her eyes. "I never want to see your face again. If I do, I will kill you without a second thought."

I stood up and took Eric's hand. Millie and Liam grabbed Lemme, and we headed for the door.

"Oh! And one more thing," I called back to Nikki. "We will stop the virus. So you might as well change your plans now. Do something productive with that science brain of yours. Frankenstein, really? Wow. If that doesn't make me a believer, I don't know what will."

"*This body is nice, Blanchmains. Thank you,*" the demon said in my mind. I glanced at her before we walked out.

You make it count, do you understand me? Destroy them and make it hurt. Don't make me regret putting you in that body.

I sat in the back of Millie's SUV with Lemme, and Eric followed us in his car. She lay out on the backseats, her head in my lap.

"I am *so* sorry," I said quietly as I stroked her hair. "I don't know if I will ever be able to make it better, but I am damn well going to try. First, we're going to get you fixed up."

Lemme coughed. "It doesn't feel bad. That means it's bad, right?"

"No! No, we're taking you to Liam's doctor right now. You will be okay." I tapped on the passenger seat where Liam sat. "She will be okay. You said!"

"Dude, you are never going to believe what she had in her lab!" Lemme began. "It was like something out of a movie. A *mermaid*, dude. A living, breathing mermaid in a giant tank!"

"She's delirious," I said. "Hurry up!"

Lemme grabbed my arm and squeezed. "I know what I saw. And we have to go get her. She did this mind meld thing where she spoke to me in my head without actually speaking, and she told me how dangerous these people are. She helped me keep it together. We can't just leave her there!"

I stroked her hair again. "We will. Let's just get you fixed up first."

I was speechless when we drove up to a garage in the east end of the city. Like the type of garage where they fix cars. It looked too fancy to be a chop shop, but what did I know. I was so worried about Lemme it didn't matter as long as they fixed her.

Two big burly guys came over to the car; they helped me get out then turned their attention to Lemme. Together they gently picked up Lemme and brought her inside. I followed them without thinking or worrying where anyone else was.

We walked through to the very back, where behind a wood door was a clean and lovely medical clinic with state-of-the-art equipment. Once the door closed behind us, it was like we were in a completely different place.

The men helped Lemme up onto an examination table and immediately got to work. He turned and looked at me after a few minutes, motioning over to a group of chairs that were up against a far wall. Eventually, I went and sat. Standing in the middle room like an idiot just made me look weird.

Millie, Eric, and Liam came in a short time later. Millie and Eric sat on each side of me, and Liam went over and spoke with the doctor. I could not see what he was doing. I was literally sitting on the edge of my seat with anticipation. The cold plastic chair was extremely uncomfortable, and my hands were gripped on the sides so tight I worried I might snap it in half. Millie and Eric did not try to soothe me. We all just quietly waited to see what would happen.

Liam came over to us a few minutes later. He knelt down in front of me, his expression made me immediately scared.

"What? What's wrong? She's going to be okay, right?" I blubbered out, trying not to hyperventilate.

"She'll be fine. It's not very deep. But she came very close. Another few centimetres and that would have been a different story," he said. I bent over and put my head between my knees, bursting into tears.

"Thank God," I finally managed when I sat upright. "And thank you for bringing her here. I don't know how I will ever repay you. Do you like cookies? I can send you some cookies. I promise I won't bake them myself."

Liam laughed, putting a hand on my shoulder. "Don't worry. But you know what you will have to do, don't you? Do you know what this means?"

I felt Millie's body tense. Eric reached out and grabbed my hand.

"Those rules don't apply to her. She doesn't know how our world works," Millie told him.

"What rules? What do you mean?" I asked no one in particular.

Eric sighed loudly. "What he's getting at is that some people would take what Bliss did as an act of aggression. And it would mean...."

"If she was a wolf, what she did would mean that I would hunt her and kill her if I was in your shoes." Liam's dark eyes remained locked with mine as he spoke. "It is an act of war in our world, Camille. I hope you understand that."

I put my hand on his shoulder and smiled. I thought

for a second about telling them what I did, about the demon that was now in Bliss's body because of me. Considering how they felt about what she did to Lemme, maybe they would understand.

I kept eye contact with Liam, I wanted to make sure he knew how much his advice meant to me."I understand. Her act of aggression will not go unnoticed. I promise."

12.

The next day I woke up early, ready to get back to my normal life. Lemme was home safe, fixed up, and healing. The demon had a body. Nikki and the Kinkaid's were out of our hair, for now.

I woke up and got ready, whistling as I went downstairs. Ted was cooking breakfast, and Cuddy was already at the table in the kitchen, chatting away. My normal, wonderfully weird family.

"Good morning," I said happily, kissing them both on the cheek as I sat down. I had never been so happy to just sit in the kitchen and listen to people talk.

"Good morning." Ted handed me a plate. "You're in a good mood."

"Yep. Ready to start the day."

"This have anything to do with your evening with Eric?"

I smiled and shrugged my shoulders. "You all got a

policy about employees dating?"

Cuddy laughed. "Considering the fact that Dad dated Ram—"

"You *what*!" I exclaimed.

"You never told her?" Cuddy asked him. He smiled mischievously at me, and I was reminded of his five-year-old little face. I remembered the day he called me Cas for the first time. I was so happy because he finally said something close to my name.

"My dating life doesn't concern either of you." Ted pointed at both of us. "Now eat your food; we're running late."

No amount of pestering would make Ted tell me about him and Ramona, and by the time we got to the office, I gave up. When we walked in the front door, Ramona looked spooked behind her desk.

I was about to ask her what was up when I saw Mr. Croft sitting in the far corner.

"Your first appointment is here," Ramona said quietly.

I smiled and nodded at them both. "Just give me a few minutes."

I rushed into my office, putting all my bags away and taking my coat off in the most orderly fashion I could. I set up my computer and put my phone in my lap as I sat down.

I wasn't sure why Mr. Croft was here. Why had Ramona not told him things just don't happen that quickly?

I buzzed Ramona and told her to send him in.

Whatever it was, I was ready for it. After last night, I felt like I could take on just about anything.

I stood up, putting my phone on my desk and smiled, holding out my hand for him to shake it.

He didn't.

He waited for Ramona to close the door then sat down, folding his hands in his lap.

"What can I do for you, Mr. Croft? I'm sorry to say that I haven't—"

"I am here to talk about my granddaughter," he said, interrupting me. "I wanted to assure you that your message was heard."

I swallowed hard. "I don't understand."

"Please, Miss Bishop. That is unnecessary. I am here to speak with you about Nicole's behaviour. She did not understand the magnitude of her actions or the situation. I am here to express my deepest apologies and extend an olive branch."

I was completely speechless. If my math was correct, this man was close to 240 years old. But I could be off. He could be older.

"It's–it's an honour to meet you, Dr. Frankenstein," I finally said.

"Yes, yes. I am pleased that we can now speak freely. I believe we could have a mutually beneficial relationship, as my granddaughter attempted to discuss, but failed miserably," he began. "I assure you that nonsense they did with the poor young woman, and that heinous act they committed at the university, will not go unpunished. Mr. Kinkaid and I spoke about it at great length. Institutes of higher learning should be treated with more respect. My granddaughter is a bright girl but does not understand the need to be diplomatic. And the Kinkaid boys are…well, they're Neanderthals."

Before I could say anything he continued, "Mr. Kinkaid does not know I am here. He believes it is best to keep our distance, where I believe, with your particular skill set, we could use your services and make you quite wealthy."

"And what skill set is that, Doctor?" I asked.

"You have unique abilities, not just magical ones. You can help us locate people that we need to further our research."

"I won't be your own personal bloodhound. I won't help you hurt anyone."

"Oh, I am sorry. I believe you misunderstand me. I have no intentions of hurting anyone." He looked down his nose at me, as if the notion disgusted him.

"I'm confused."

"There are some people I need to locate. Immortals. Learning more about them will help further my research," he said flatly, clearly irritated that I had not clued in to his subtleties.

"I know nothing of any immortals, Doctor. I am not sure how much help I could be."

He smiled and pulled a business card from inside his suit coat pocket, handing it in my direction. "Speak to your people. Clearly you are not informed about the world you live in. If you are interested, please get in touch with me."

When I did not reach out to take it from him, he put the card on my desk, stood, and walked out.

I scrambled over the top of my desk, almost falling on my face as I followed him. I wanted to see if he was floating. He smiled and waved to Ramona as he left, getting into a black SUV that was waiting outside.

"Well fuck me gently with a chainsaw," I mumbled to myself as I walked back to my office. Eric stood in my doorway.

"Who was that?" he asked.

"*That* was Dr. Frankenstein. We need to talk about immortals. This whole thing just upped the weird factor."

13.

I pulled my pyjamas out of the drawer and something fell out, making a thumping sound when it hit my carpet.

I was surprised to see one of the little tins where Jesse kept his drug accessories spill out on the floor. I hadn't even known it was there.

What else did he have stashed around my room?

I pictured Jesse's face in my mind, and my vision went milky; my eyes felt like they were vibrating in my head.

I knew what it meant and my heart sank. The idea of facing him now made me want to vomit. How much of the truth did I want to tell him?

"How did I get here?" I heard him before I saw him. I tried hard to level out my breathing.

"Sorry. I didn't do it on purpose," I replied.

"Camille?"

"Yeah, Jesse. It's me."

"Thank God! Can you explain to me what the hell is happening?"

"Yeah, I can, but I don't know if you'll believe me."

I'm not going to cry.

"Can you look at me?" he asked.

I took a deep breath, then turned towards him.

He looked better than he had in the days before he died. He wasn't wearing a hat or his hoodie, just a plain white t-shirt and jeans. His hair was short and uneven. He looked healthy for a ghost, the healthiest I had seen him look in years.

"You're...you are...you're dead, Jesse. And you're here because I summoned you. Accidently, but I still summoned you."

"I already knew about the dead part. But you 'summoned' me? Since when can you do that?"

"It's all new to me, hence the accidently part. Long story. The Coles notes version is that my mom bound my powers and a chain of events...unbound them."

"Wow. That's heavy."

"You don't even know the half of it. I am surprised you believe me."

"How could I not? Look at what you did," he began. "Were you there? When I died?"

"No. We were broken up, remember?"

He examined my face. "Right. I forgot. I'm sorry, Camille."

"Sorry for what? I dumped you."

"Sorry for everything. I was horrible to you. I took

you for granted. I treated you like a piece of furniture, for no other reason than I could. I know you probably don't believe me, but I did love you in my own warped way. That is my one regret, and explains *a lot* about what has happened since I died. You deserve better, and I wish I could give it to you."

I sat down on my bed and burst into tears. I tried to form words, but I just sounded like a bumbling mess.

It took a few minutes, but I was finally able to take a few deep breaths and calm down.

"I want to believe you," I blubbered out, "but it's been too many times."

"I'm dead, Camille. It's not like I can cheat on you now."

"So that would be the only time you are truly sorry? When you can't do anything else? Of course. You're only sorry because it clears your conscience, and now all you have is time to think."

He put his face in his hands, shaking his head in frustration. "That totally came out wrong. I get why you wouldn't believe me, but I am truly sorry, okay? I hope one day you will find it in your heart to forgive me."

I wiped my tears on my hand. "Thank you for saying that."

"Does this mean we get to spend eternity alone together?"

I chuckled. "Not exactly. I am new to this summoning thing, but you don't stay forever. You go back and forth."

"Oh." He sounded disappointed. "Will you ever

summon me again?"

"Of course," I replied. "Jesse?"

"Yeah, babe?"

"What's it like?"

"What's what like?"

"Death. Dying. What's it like?"

"Truthfully, I don't remember. I remember being at a bar. Burnt Offerings. I remember talking to a girl with dark hair who reminded me of you, but she wasn't...then I got drunk and things are fuzzy. I remember being in bed here with you, then waking up outside."

"Why did you go to Burnt Offerings?"

"Bucky wanted to. Some friend of Bliss's who he would not stop talking about. He was obsessed with her. She was a sorority sister or some shit. She was there one night with some friends. I was shocked a girl like that would give him the time of day. But they acted like he was the chosen one or some shit."

"He's dead too." I had a lot of questions about this 'sorority sister' and Bucky being the chosen one, but I wasn't sure Jesse could answer them. My first reaction was to be disgusted that Bliss could use her brother for some *bruja* craziness. But if it was a family thing, Bucky would have been well aware of what she was.

His devastation was hard to hide."What? How did he die? Who?"

"From what I know, Lucia Kinkaid had his face bashed in because of Bliss."

"I told you. Bliss is trouble with a capital T."

"I know. I found out the hard way. Lucia was trying to send a message that Bliss belonged to her. Then Bliss shot her in the head and ended up getting claimed by Tobias Kinkaid. I'm not sure they know she killed Lucia though."

"How do you know? Bliss is a fantastic liar."

"I was there when she shot Lucia. And yes, I know exactly how fantastic of a liar she is."

"Well, okay then. Is she still your friend?"

"Fuck no. Why?"

"Because she made a pass at me. More than once."

"She said you tried to recruit her for porn and your brothel."

"That's absolute crap! Bucky would have killed me... wait, did Bucky kill me?"

"Not to my knowledge."

"How did I die?"

"I'm not entirely sure. At first they thought you OD'd. But now Kiera is investigating it as a homicide. Or a possible homicide. I'm not sure what the term is."

"How's Rollo?"

"Not sure. He was nasty to me right after he found out. I haven't spoken to him much since."

"Did he mention Amanda?"

I groaned. "No. She came with him to your funeral. Other than that, I don't know."

"I'm not asking because I want to know. I'm asking because she is a toxic goddamn succubus. She was drugging me."

"I don't understand."

"She was putting drugs in my food and drinks if I didn't see her for a few days, and when I got sick I would end up crawling back to her. It's fucked up."

Part of me wanted to laugh. Only Jesse could pick up a nut job like that. "How did you figure that out?"

"I caught her red-handed. That was shortly after you and I broke up and was one of the reasons I got crackhead skinny. Rollo isn't smart enough to figure that out."

"That's his problem, not yours. Or mine."

"Could you talk to him?"

I laughed loudly, and Jesse looked taken aback. "Absolutely not. He was horrible to me and said some evil shit that I cannot forgive. Besides, what do I tell him? That Jesse's ghost sent me?"

"Wait, back up. You said my brothel. What are you talking about?"

"I have video of you and Amanda in a brothel downtown."

"Were we...?"

"She was banging an old dude then gave you the payment."

He hesitated. "Can you show me?"

I opened up my laptop and found the video. Part of me didn't want to show him, didn't want to rip open that wound that was starting to heal. Another part of me wanted to see his face when he watched it. I wanted a real honest explanation. And an apology.

I pushed play and put the laptop on my bed beside me.

He sat down beside the laptop and watched the screen closely. Sitting that close to him and not being able to touch him was strange.

Why couldn't I touch him?

I reached out and tried to touch his shoulder, but my fingers easily passed through like he was air. I was overwhelmed with a deep and terrible sadness for him.

 He was my first love, my first kiss, my first everything. While I may not have wanted to be his girlfriend anymore, I wanted him to have a regular life. I wanted him to get clean and move on and be a real person. Have a life that his little brother, or his future children, could be proud of.

Any life at all.

"I can't imagine what you must have thought when you saw this," he said a few minutes after the video ended. "Where were you?"

"Parked out front with Q. She was also driving the vehicle when I found you and Amanda and we broke up."

"Oh," he stopped, looking across the room as if someone was there. He listened to whatever they said then turned back to me.

He reached out to touch my knee and his fingers passed right through. He looked at his hand with a mixture of shock and annoyance. His eyes turned up to me then, and my heart sank. It was hard not to be sad for him, even with the drugs and the other women and everything.

"Listen, the powers that be want me to tell you

something," he said. "They want you to know that if you are not careful, the darkness will consume you."

"That's a little cryptic. Who are the powers that be?"

"They run the other place I go to. The middle ground is what some of the others call it."

"Thanks for the tip. I get loads of cryptic weirdness now that I have powers. I should write a handbook or something."

"So if you have powers, does that mean other things exist, like vampires and werewolves?"

"To make a long story short, yes. The Kinkaid's are vampires."

"Cool," he looked away again. "I have to go. Will you summon me again, Camille?"

I smiled. I liked to think I would summon him on purpose. Hopefully, after the first time, it wouldn't hurt as bad.

"Yeah, Jesse. I will."

"I want to know what happened to me. Will you tell me?"

"Sure. If you really want to know."

He tried to smile, but it was hard when his bottom lip was quivering.

"So I guess this is goodbye?" he said quietly.

I held out my hand and he put his just above so it looked like we were touching.

"No, it's not goodbye. More like smell you later." A tear rolled down my cheek.

"It's weird to be here like this with you and not be

able to kiss you goodbye."

"I know," I replied. I blinked and he was gone.

In that moment, I felt completely alone, and my grief finally caught up with me. Moving my laptop to my desk, I lay down on my bed and put my hand out flat where he had been sitting. The warmth of the laptop gave the illusion of what could have been.

At least I got to say goodbye this time.

My phone rang a little while later. I wasn't sure how long I had been lying there. I had been thinking about all the things Jesse could have done, if he had gotten to live. The life he could have had if things had been different. If I wasn't the goddamn prophecy girl.

I tried to sound chipper. "Hello?"

"Hey! Were you sleeping?" Eric's voice immediately made me feel better.

"No, I'm good. What's up?"

"I can hear it in your voice, Camille. Spill it."

"I accidentally summoned Jesse."

He was silent for a moment. "How did that go?"

"I don't know. I don't think I'll ever get used to talking to people I really cared about after they've died."

"How did he handle it?"

"Better than I expected. Didn't make it any less weird though. It'll be good preparation for when I talk to my mom."

"Are you okay?"

"Yeah. I'm okay."

"Hopefully things have calmed down and life can return to our new normal."

I laughed. "New normal?"

"Yeah, this life will get less crazy, I promise. And I'm here for you."

"Thank you," I said. "And I sure as fuck hope you're right. I wish you were here."

"I can be."

My ears perked up. "I don't know what Ted would say."

"He won't even see me. I can astral project myself to you."

"What? What the hell is that?"

"The simplest explanation is that I can project an image of myself there with you. It's still me, I can hear you and everything, but my physical body is not there."

"Shut the front door! For real?"

"Absolutely. One of the cool parts of being the Merlin. We'll hang up now. You get comfortable, and I will be there shortly."

I was grinning ear to ear. "Okay. See you soon."

"See you soon," he replied, and we both hung up.

Grabbing my discarded pyjamas from the floor, I took a few minutes to make myself presentable after the crying. Mascara trails running down my cheeks were not a good look. Teddy bear in hand, I positioned myself on the bed in such a way that he had plenty of room. After closing my eyes for only a second, my senses were filled with Eric's warm woodsy scent. When I opened my eyes, he was there, but he shimmered white at his edges. He smiled at me and stroked my cheek. It felt like the soft touch of a feather.

"Thank you," I said quietly to him. He stroked my hair, and then gently wrapped his arm around me. It felt like a blanket of him was covering me, his smell all around me.

"This is good. If I can't have you with me, this is good too," I told him. He said nothing. I knew he could hear me, but I wondered if he could reply.

"I hope you know how much I want to be with you. And I don't just mean physically. These last few weeks with you have been some of the best in my life, even with the chaos." I closed my eyes. "I am so glad you are part of my new normal."

14.

The next day, I slept in late. I hadn't slept that good in years. I had fallen asleep in Eric's arms. He wasn't there when I woke up, but I was okay with that. I had sent him a thank you text, letting him know that I wanted to see him again. Soon.

I had a rare free Saturday morning to myself, so I decided to look through my dad's files. There were multiple boxes, but I was particularly drawn to the one that happened to be on my desk. It had a weird eerie glow to it that made me think it was important.

I opened the box and began taking files out. I was impressed with my father's organizational system. Each file contained information about an object, mostly rare antiques, including photos and various details.

I scanned through the detailed purchase histories of a few of them and saw they were each bought by The Kinkaid Group or a 'proxy bidder on behalf of'. I tried to pull out all the purchase histories and found that some were stolen, a few from museums and a few from private citizens.

At first, I was surprised that someone like Elliot Kinkaid would be such an avid collector, but when I looked further at the files and the randomness of the objects, I couldn't help but wonder what the connection was that my dad would not have seen. There were no notes, no reports or anything that expressed what my dad thought, or if he even figured out the significance of these items. He had kept a notebook—one of those small black ones like detectives kept in the movies, that could have contained such personal observations—but it was nowhere to be found.

Him not seeing a connection was unheard of. Some felt that William Bishop was a brilliant detective. One of the greats. But then you have to factor in my mother. She was smart and clearly did not want us involved in this life. What lengths would she have gone to to keep us out of it? And is her grand deception one of the reasons they did not see Kinkaid coming and got killed?

My dad never made the connection between these items. Had my mom made sure of that because they had some great magical significance?

My dad had also started a file on the proxy bidder, who he believed was connected to the robberies. He had very limited information, only a vague description of a woman. Which seemed odd considering how thorough my Dad always was. And that meant one of two things:

Either he did not think she was important, or he could not find any information about her. A few blurry surveillance photos from an auction house told me she was tall, probably close to six feet. She would be hard to miss.

I got a pad of paper off my desk and started making lists that I could use for quick reference. My Father's files were meticulously organized, so my list consisted of the file number and a short description of the item—just so I didn't have to dig around all the time—along with a list of the auction houses used and museums and private citizens robbed. I had a good place to start.

One item in particular made me pause. It was stolen from a private citizen named Damien Barnhill III from his Toronto condo that he only used while travelling, his primary residence being in London, England. The country of origin was listed as England, and I was surprised it was not returned there. The item was a sword, a rather large one, with an intricate handle that was engraved with various designs.

Something about it looked familiar. I had a flash of my own hand on the sword, and I could feel water splashing around my ankles. I shook my head quickly and tried to snap myself out of it. The memory disappeared, but the great weight of the sword in my hand lingered.

I continued reading the file about the sword. My father had gathered quite a lot of information about it specifically. It seemed that Barnhill had made several attempts to purchase the sword and failed, and also tried several lawsuits claiming he could prove the sword belonged to one of his ancestors and that he should have it by right. He eventually purchased the sword at auction for an obscene amount of money, beating out the female mystery bidder by $400K.

Who would pay that kind of money for a sword?

It had to be a pretty serious sword for that kind of money. The magic so highly sought after, people would pay in extremes and steal to get it.

What kind of magical sword would be that interesting?

Do you believe yet, dummy?

No. No way.

That took way *too long, Camille.*

Could I be looking at Excalibur?

Bing! Bing! Bing! Give the woman a prize!

Welcome to your new normal, Camille.

ACKNOWLEDGMENTS.

Thank you RM Gilmore for your support, friendship, and being the best damn designer on the whole planet.

Thank you Tara Dawn for your editing magic, your kindness, and your friendship.

Without the two of you, this book would not have come together. I would be quite lost without the both of you. Thank you for your awesomeness, and showing me what true friendship is all about. I am beyond lucky to call both of you my friends.

Thank you to my husband Michael for believing in me even when I don't believe in myself. I love you.

This story took longer to come together than the previous book, but I think the end product turned out pretty cool.

I hope you all enjoy it.

ABOUT RAVIN TIJA MAURICE

Ravin Tija Maurice lives in Mississauga, Ontario, Canada with her husband and daughter.

Her books span several time periods and feature a diverse cast of characters, all with a paranormal twist. She loves to binge watch television shows, has a large collection of stuffed animals, and is a history geek. A lifelong writer, she is constantly trying to find ways to grow and learn new skills.